FOUR SQUARE JANE

FOUR SQUARE JANE

EDGAR WALLACE

WILDSIDE PRESS

INTRODUCTION

DARRELL SCHWEITZER

The claim is encountered variously: Once upon a time, Edgar Wallace novels made up 25% of all books, including Bibles, sold in 1) Great Britain; 2) the English-speaking world; 3) the entire world. Whatever the truth, it is certain that Wallace (1875-1932) was one of the most prolific and successful writers of all time. He was born into poverty, left school at 12, and worked a variety of jobs until he became a newspaper reporter, not always a successful one, apparently, because several lawsuits resulted from the inaccuracy of his reporting. In the course of his reporting career, he was a war correspondent during the Boer War and traveled to the Congo to report on Belgian atrocities there.

Initially inspired by Kipling, whom he had met in Cape Town in 1898, he released a book of ballads, *The Mission That Failed!*, in 1898. He found his true literary calling with the first of his "thrillers," *Four Just Men* in 1905. Initially he had to found a company himself to publish the book. Sales were good, but the company went broke. This set a pattern seen throughout Wallace's life, that he had and lost several fortunes and was as often deeply in debt as rolling in money, but he always felt that he could pull himself out of trouble just writing a few more novels, many of which he dictated onto a wax-cylinder recorder in unbroken 72-hour stretches. Certainly, after his first novel, he never had to self-publish again. At the height of his fame publishers were clamoring for anything he could write, as fast as he could write it, and for Wallace that meant a lot, and very fast. He produced over 170 novels and many volumes of short stories. Over 160 films were based on his work, although he often sold film rights to his books quickly, and outright (for a lump sum, without royalties) whenever he needed quick cash. In 1931, once again in debt, much of it to bookies, he moved to Hollywood and began working as a "script doctor" for RKO, in addition to writing original screenplays. He died of undiagnosed diabetes in 1932, having just completed a rough draft of the script for *King Kong*. (The novel of *King Kong* was written by Delos W. Lovelace and is based on the final screenplay, which incorporated elements from Wallace's original draft.)

The great majority of Wallace's novels are crime thrillers or detective stories. His time in the Congo also gave him background material for the popular *Sanders of the Rivers* series of jungle adventures. He wrote a small amount of science fiction, most notably *Planetoid 127* (1924), which is about a man in contact with the equivalent of himself on a duplicate Earth on the other side of the Sun. It is widely reported that Wallace sold, overall, about 50 million copies of his books during his lifetime.

CHAPTER 1

Mr. Joe Lewinstein slouched to one of the long windows which gave light to his magnificent drawing-room and stared gloomily across the lawn.

The beds of geraniums and lobelias were half-obscured by a driving mist of rain, and the well-kept lawns that were the pride of his many gardeners were sodden and, in places, under water.

"Of course it had to rain today," he said bitterly.

His large and comfortable wife looked up over her glasses.

"Why, Joe," she said, "what's the good of grousing? They haven't come down for an al fresco fête; they've come down for the dance and the shooting, and anything else they can get out of us."

"Oh, shut up, Miriam," said Mr. Lewinstein irritably; "what does it matter what they're coming for? It's what I want them for myself. You don't suppose I've risen from what I was to my present position without learning anything, do you?" Mr. Lewinstein was fond of referring to his almost meteoric rise in the world of high finance, if not in the corresponding world of society. And, to do him justice, it must be added that such companies as he had promoted, and they were many, had been run on the most straightforward lines, nor had he, to use his own words, risked the money of the "widows and orphans." At least, not unnecessarily.

"It's knowing the right kind of people," he continued, "and doing them the right kind of turns that counts. It's easier to make your second million than your first, and I'm going to make it, Miriam," he added, with grim determination. "I'm going to make it, and I'm not sticking at a few thousands in the way of expenses!"

A housewifely fear lest their entertainment that night was going to cost them thousands floated through Mrs. Lewinstein's mind, but she said nothing.

"I'll bet they've never seen a ball like ours is tonight," her husband continued with satisfaction, as he turned his back on the window and came slowly towards his partner, "and the company will be worth it, Miriam, you believe me. Everybody who's anybody in the city is coming. There'll be more jewels here tonight than even I could buy."

His wife put down her paper with an impatient gesture.

"That's what I'm thinking about," she said. "I hope you know what you're doing. It's a big responsibility."

"What do you mean by responsibility?" asked Joe Lewinstein.

"All this loose money lying about," said his wife. "Don't you read the paper? Don't any of your friends tell you?"

Mr. Lewinstein burst into a peal of husky laughter.

"Oh, I know what's biting you," he said. "You're thinking of Four Square Jane."

"Four Square Jane!" said the acid Mrs. Lewinstein. "I'd give her Four Square Jane if I had her in this house!"

"She's no common burglar," said Mr. Lewinstein shaking his head, whether in admonition or admiration it was difficult to say. "My friend, Lord Belchester—my friend, Lord Belchester, told me it was an absolute mystery how his wife lost those emeralds of hers. He was very worried about it, was Belchester. He took about half the money he made out of Consolidated Grains to buy those emeralds, and they were lost about a month after he bought them. He thinks that the thief was one of his guests."

"Why do they call her Four Square Jane?" asked Mrs. Lewinstein curiously.

Her husband shrugged his shoulders.

"She always leaves a certain mark behind her, a sort of printed label with four squares, and the letter J in the middle," he said. "It was the police who called her Jane, and somehow the name has stuck."

His wife picked up the paper and put it down again, looking thoughtfully into the fire.

"And you're bringing all these people down here to stop the night, and you're talking about them being loaded up with jewellery! You've got a nerve, Joe."

Mr. Lewinstein chuckled.

"I've got a detective, too," he said. "I've asked Ross, who has the biggest private detective agency in London, to send me his best woman."

"Goodness gracious," said the dismayed Mrs. Lewinstein, "you're not having a woman here?"

"Yes, I am. She's a lady, apparently one of the best girls Ross has got. He told me that in cases like this it's much less noticeable to have a lady detective among the guests than a man. I told her to be here at seven."

Undoubtedly the Lewinstein's house-party was the most impressive affair that the county had seen. His guests were to arrive by a special train from London and were to be met at the station by a small fleet of motor cars, which he had pressed to his service from all available sources. His own car was waiting at the door ready to take him to the station to meet his "special" when a servant brought him a card.

"Miss Caroline Smith," he read. On the corner was the name of the Ross Detective Agency.

"Tell the young lady I'll see her in the library."

He found her waiting for him. A personable, pretty girl, with remarkably shrewd and clever eyes that beamed behind rimless glasses and a veil, she met him with an elusive smile that came and went like sunshine on a wintry day.

"So you're a lady detective, eh?" said Lewinstein with ponderous good humour; "you look young."

"Why, yes," said the girl, "even way home, where youth isn't any handicap, I'm looked upon as being a trifle under the limit."

"Oh, you're from America, are you?" said Mr. Lewinstein interested.

The girl nodded.

"This is my first work in England, and naturally I am rather nervous."

She had a pleasant voice, a soft drawl, which suggested to Mr. Lewinstein, who had spent some years on the other side, that she came from one of the Southern States.

"Well, I suppose you pretty well know your duties in the game to suppress this Four Square woman."

She nodded.

"That may be a pretty tough proposition. You'll give me leave to go where I like, and do practically what I like, won't you? That is essential."

"Certainly," said Mr. Lewinstein; "you will dine with us as our guest?"

"No, that doesn't work," she replied. "The time I ought to be looking round and taking notice, my attention is wholly absorbed by the man who is taking me down to dinner and wants my views on prohibition.

"So, if you please, I'd like the whole run of your house. I can be your young cousin, Miranda, from the high mountains of New Jersey. What about your servants?"

"I can trust them with my life," said Mr. Lewinstein.

She looked at him with a half-twinkle in her eyes.

"Can you tell me anything about this she-Raffles?" she asked.

"Nothing," said her host, "except that she is one of these society swells who frequent such—well, such parties as I am giving tonight. There will be a lot of ladies here—some of the best in the land—that is what makes it so difficult. As likely as not she will be one of them."

"Would you trust them all with your life?" she asked mischievously, and then going on: "I think I know your Four Square woman. Mind," she raised her hand, "I'm not going to say that I shall discover her here."

"I hope to goodness you don't," said Joe heartily.

"Or if I do find her I'm going to denounce her. Perhaps you can tell me something else about her."

Mr. Lewinstein shook his head.

"The only thing I know is that when she's made a haul, she usually leaves behind a mark."

"That I know," said the girl nodding. "She does that in order that suspicion shall not fall upon the servants."

The girl thought a moment, tapping her teeth with a pencil, then she said:

"Whatever I do, Mr. Lewinstein, you must not regard as remarkable. I have set my mind on capturing Four Square Jane, and starting my career in England with a big flourish of silver trumpets." She smiled so charmingly that Mrs. Lewinstein in the doorway raised her eyebrows.

"It is time you were going, Joseph," she said severely. "What am I to do with this young woman?"

"Let somebody show her her room," said the temporarily flustered Mr. Lewinstein, and hurried out to the waiting car.

Mrs. Lewinstein rang the bell. She had no interest in detectives, especially pretty detectives of twenty-three.

Adchester Manor House was a large establishment, but it was packed to its utmost capacity to accommodate the guests who arrived that night.

All Mrs. Lewinstein had said—that these pretty women and amusing men had been lured into Buckinghamshire with a lively hope of favours to come—might be true. Joe Lewinstein was not only a power in the City, with the control of four great corporations, but the Lewinstein interests stretched from Colorado to Vladivostock.

It was a particularly brilliant party which sat down to dinner that night, and if Mr. Lewinstein swelled a little with pride, that pride was certainly justified. On his right sat Lady Ovingham, a thin woman with the prettiness that consists chiefly in huge appealing eyes and an almost alarming pallor of skin. Her appearance greatly belied her character, for she was an unusually able business woman, and had partnered Mr. Lewinstein in some of his safer speculations. An arm covered from wrist to elbow with diamond bracelets testified to the success of these ventures in finance, for Lady Ovingham had a way of investing her money in diamonds, for she knew that these stones would not suddenly depreciate in value.

The conversation was animated and, in many cases, hilarious, for Mr. Lewinstein had mixed his guests as carefully as his butler had mixed the cocktails, and both things helped materially towards the success of the evening.

It was towards the end of the dinner that the first disagreeable incident occurred. His butler leant over him, ostensibly to pour out a glass of wine, and whispered:

"That young lady that came this afternoon, sir, has been taken ill."

"Ill!" said Mr. Lewinstein in dismay. "What happened?"

"She complained of a bad headache, was seized with tremblings, and had to be taken up to her room," said the butler in a low voice.

"Send into the village for the doctor."

"I did, sir," said the man, "but the doctor had been called away to London on an important consultation."

Mr. Lewinstein frowned. Then a little gleam of relief came to him. The detective had asked him not to be alarmed at anything that might happen. Possibly this was a ruse for her own purpose. She ought to have told him though, he complained to himself.

"Very good, wait till dinner is over," he said.

When that function was finished, and the guests had reached the coffee and cigarette stage before entering the big ballroom or retiring to their cards, Mr. Lewinstein climbed to the third floor to the tiny bedroom which had been allocated by his lady wife as being adequate for a lady detective.

He knocked at the door.

"Come in," said a faint voice.

The girl was lying on the bed, covered with an eiderdown quilt, and she was shivering.

"Don't touch me," she said. "I don't know what's the matter with me even."

"Good Lord!" said Mr. Lewinstein in dismay, "you're not really ill, are you?"

"I'm afraid so; I'm awfully sorry. I don't know what has happened to me, and I have a feeling that my illness is not wholly accidental. I was feeling well until I had a cup of tea, which was brought to my room, when suddenly I was taken with these shivers. Can you get me a doctor?"

"I'll do my best," said Mr. Lewinstein, for he had a kindly heart.

He went downstairs a somewhat anxious man. If, as the girl seemed to suggest, she had been doped, that presupposed the presence in the house either of Four Square Jane or one of her working partners. He reached the hall to find the butler waiting.

"Excuse me, sir," said the butler, "but rather a fortunate thing has happened. A gentleman who has run short of petrol came up to the house to borrow a supply——"

"Well?" said Mr. Lewinstein.

"Well, sir, he happens to be a doctor," said the butler. "I asked him to see you, sir."

"Fine," said Mr. Lewinstein enthusiastically, "that's a good idea of yours. Bring him into the library."

The stranded motorist, a tall young man, came in full of apologies.

"I say, it's awfully good of you to let me have this juice," he said. "The fact is, my silly ass of a man packed me two empty tins."

"Delighted to help you, doctor," said Mr. Lewinstein genially; "and now perhaps you can help me."

The young man looked at the other suspiciously.

"You haven't anybody ill, have you?" he asked, "I promised my partner I wouldn't look at a patient for three months. You see," he explained, "I've had rather a heavy time lately, and I'm a bit run down."

"You'd be doing us a real kindness if you'd look at this young lady," said Mr. Lewinstein earnestly. "I don't know what to make of her, doctor."

"Setheridge is my name," said the doctor. "All right, I'll look at your patient. It was ungracious of me to pull a face I suppose. Where is she? Is she one of your guests by the way? I seem to have butted in on a party."

"Not exactly," Mr. Lewinstein hesitated, "she is—er—a visitor."

He led the way up to the room, and the young man walked in and looked at the shivering girl with the easy confident smile of the experienced practitioner.

"Hullo," he said, "what's the matter with you?"

He took her wrist in his hand and looked at his watch, and Mr. Lewinstein, standing in the open doorway, saw him frown. He bent down and examined the eyes, then pulled up the sleeve of his patient's dress and whistled.

"Is it serious?" she asked anxiously.

"Not very, if you are taken care of; though you may lose some of that hair," he said, with a smile at the brown mop on the pillow.

"What is it?" she asked.

"Scarlet fever, my young friend."

"Scarlet fever!" It was Mr. Lewinstein who gasped the words. "You don't mean that?"

The doctor walked out and joined him on the landing, closing the door behind him.

"It's scarlet fever, all right. Have you any idea where she was infected?"

"Scarlet fever," moaned Mr. Lewinstein; "and I've got the house full of aristocracy!"

"Well, the best thing you can do is to keep the aristocracy in ignorance of the fact. Get the girl out of the house."

"But how? How?" wailed Mr. Lewinstein.

The doctor scratched his head.

"Of course, I don't want to do it," he said slowly; "but I can't very well leave a girl in a mess like this. May I use your telephone?"

"Certainly, use anything you like; but, for goodness' sake, get the girl away!"

Mr. Lewinstein showed him the library, where the young man called up a number and gave some instructions. Apparently his telephone interview was satisfactory, for he came back to the hall, where Mr. Lewinstein was nervously drumming his fingers on the polished surface of a table, with a smile.

"I can get an ambulance out here, but not before three in the morning," he said; "anyway, that will suit us, because your guests will be abed and asleep by then, and most of the servants also, I suppose. And we can get her out without anybody being the wiser."

"I'm awfully obliged to you, doctor," said Mr. Lewinstein, "anything you like to charge me——"

The doctor waved fees out of consideration.

Then a thought occurred to Mr. Lewinstein.

"Doctor, could that disease be communicated to the girl by means of a drug, or anything?"

"Why do you ask?" said the other quickly.

"Well, because she was all right till she had a cup of tea. I must take you into my confidence," he said, lowering his voice. "She is a detective, brought down here to look after my guests. There have been a number of robberies committed lately by a woman who calls herself 'Four Square Jane,' and, to be on the safe side, I had this girl down to protect the property of my friends. When I saw her before dinner she was as well as you or I; then a cup of tea was given to her, and immediately she had these shiverings."

The doctor nodded thoughtfully.

"It is curious you should say that," he said; "for though she has the symptoms of scarlet fever, she has others which are not usually to be found in scarlet fever cases. Do you suggest that this woman, this Four Square person, is in the house?"

"Either she or her agent," said Mr. Lewinstein. "She has several people who work with her by all accounts."

"And you believe that she has given this girl a drug to put her out of the way?"

"That's my idea."

"By jove!" said the young man, "that's rather a scheme. Well, anyway, there will be plenty of people knocking about tonight, so your guests will be safe for tonight."

The girl had been housed in the servants' wing, but fortunately in a room isolated from all the others. Mr. Lewinstein made several trips upstairs during the course of the evening, saw through the open door the doctor sitting by the side of the bed, and was content. His guests retired towards one o'clock and the agitated Mrs. Lewinstein, to whom the news of the catastrophe had been imparted, having been successfully induced to go to bed, Mr. Lewinstein breathed more freely.

At half-past one he made his third visit to the door of the sick room, for he, himself, was not without dread of infection, and saw through the open door the doctor sitting reading a book near the head of the bed.

He stole quietly down, so quietly that he almost surprised a slim figure that was stealing along the darkened corridor whence opened the bedrooms of the principal guests.

She flattened herself into a recess, and he passed her so closely that she could have touched him. She waited until he had disappeared, and then crossed to one of the doors and felt gingerly at the key-hole. The occupant had made the mistake of locking the door and taking out the key, and in a second she had inserted one of her own, and softly turning it, had tip-toed into the room.

She stood listening; there was a steady breathing, and she made her way to the dressing-table, where her deft fingers began a rapid but silent search. Presently she found what she wanted, a smooth leather case, and shook it gently. She was not a minute in the room before she was out again, closing the door softly behind her.

She had half-opened the next door before she saw that there was a light in the room and she stood motionless in the shadow of the doorway. On the far side of the bed the little table-lamp was still burning, and it would, she reflected, have helped her a great deal, if only she could have been sure that the person who was lying among the frilled pillows of the bed was really asleep. She waited rigid, and with all her senses alert for five minutes, till the sound of regular breathing from the bed reassured her. Then she slipped forward to the dressing-table. Here, her task was easy. No less than a dozen little velvet and leather cases lay strewn on the silk cover. She opened them noiselessly one by one, and put their glittering contents into her pocket, leaving the cases as they had been.

As she was handling the last of the jewels a thought struck her, and she peered more closely at the sleeping figure. A thin pretty woman, it seemed in the half-light. So this was the businesslike Lady Ovingham. She left the room as noiselessly as she had entered it, and more quickly, and tried the next door in the passage.

This one had not been locked.

It was Mrs. Lewinstein's own room, but she was not sleeping quietly. The door had been left open for her lord, who had made a promise to see his wife to make arrangements for the morrow. This promise he had quite forgotten in his perturbation. There was a little safe let into the wall, and the keys were hanging in the lock; for Mr. Lewinstein, who, being a prudent, careful man, was in the habit of depositing his diamond studs every night.

The girl's fingers went into the interior of the safe, and presently she found what she wanted. Mrs. Lewinstein stopped breathing heavily, grunted, and turned, and the girl stood stock-still. Presently the snoring recommenced, and she stole out into the corridor.

As she closed each door she stopped only long enough to press a small label against the surface of the handle before she passed on to the next room.

Downstairs in the library, Mr. Lewinstein heard the soft purr of a motor car, and rose with a sigh of relief. Only his butler had been let into the secret, and that sleepy retainer, who was dozing in one of the hall chairs, heard the sound with as great relief as his employer. He opened the big front door.

Outside was a motor-ambulance from which two men had descended. They pulled out a stretcher and a bundle of blankets, and made their way into the hall.

"I will show you the way," said Mr. Lewinstein. "You will make as little noise as possible, please."

He led the procession up the carpeted stairs, and came at last to the girl's room.

"Oh, here you are," said the doctor, yawning. "Set the stretcher by the side of the bed. You had better stand away some distance, Mr. Lewinstein," he said, and that gentleman obeyed with alacrity.

Presently the door opened and the stretcher came out, bearing the blanket-enveloped figure of the girl, her face just visible, and she favoured Mr. Lewinstein with a pathetic smile as she passed.

The stairs were negotiated without any difficulty by the attendants, and carefully the stretcher was pushed into the interior of the ambulance.

"That's all right," said the doctor; "if I were you I would have that bedroom locked up and fumigated tomorrow."

"I'm awfully obliged to you, doctor. If you will give me your address I would like to send you a cheque."

"Oh, rubbish," said the other cheerfully, "I am only too happy to serve you. I will go into the village to pick up my car and get back to town myself."

"Where will you take this young woman?" asked Mr. Lewinstein.

"To the County Fever Hospital," replied the other carelessly. "That's where you're taking her, isn't it?"

"Yes, sir," said one of the attendants.

Mr. Lewinstein waited on the steps until the red lights of the car had disappeared, then stepped inside with the sense of having managed a very difficult situation rather well.

"That will do for the night," he said to the butler. "Thank you for waiting up."

He found himself walking, with a little smile on his lips, along the corridor to his own room.

As he was passing his wife's door he stumbled over something. Stooping, he picked up a case. There was an electric switch close by, and he flooded the corridor with light.

"Jumping Moses!" he gasped, for the thing he held in his hand was his wife's jewel case.

He made a run for her door, and was just gripping the handle, when the label there caught his eye, and he stared in hopeless bewilderment at the sign of Four Square Jane.

* * * *

An ambulance stopped at a cross-road, where a big car was waiting, and the patient, who had long since thrown off her blankets, came out. She pulled after her a heavy bag, which one of the two attendants lifted for her and placed in the car. The doctor was sitting at the wheel.

"I was afraid I was going to keep you waiting," he said. "I only just got here in time."

He turned to the attendant.

"I shall see you tomorrow, Jack."

"Yes, doctor," replied the other.

He touched his hat to Four Square Jane, and walked back to the ambulance, waiting only to change the number plates before he drove away in the opposite direction to London.

"Are you ready?" asked the doctor.

"Quite ready," said the girl, dropping in by his side. "You were late, Jim. I nearly pulled a real fit when I heard they'd sent for the local sawbones."

"You needn't have worried," said the man at the wheel, as he started the car forward. "I got a pal to wire calling him to London. Did you get the stuff?"

"Yards of it," said Four Square Jane laconically. "There will be some sad hearts in Lewinstein's house tomorrow."

He smiled.

"By the way," she said, "that lady detective Ross sent, how far did she get?"

"As far as the station," said the doctor, "which reminds me that I forgot to let her out of the garage where I locked her."

"Let her stay," said Four Square Jane. "I hate the idea of she-detectives, anyway—it's so unwomanly."

CHAPTER 2

The chairman of the Bloxley Road Hospital for Women took his seat at the head of the table, with a grim nod of recognition for his colleagues, and a more respectful inclination of his head for that eminent surgeon, Sir John Denham, who was attending this momentous meeting of the Governors by special invitation.

Doctor Parsons, the chairman, pushed aside a little brown paper parcel which lay on his blotting pad, and which he saw, after a cursory glance, was addressed to himself. Presumably this contained the new vaccine tubes which he had ordered from the research laboratory. He cast a swift glance from left to right, smiling a little bitterly at the glum faces of the staff.

"Well, gentlemen," he said, "Bloxley Road Hospital looks like closing."

"Is it as bad as that, sir?" asked one of the surgeons with a troubled face, and Dr. Parsons nodded.

"I suppose you didn't have any luck, Sir John?"

Sir John Denham shook his head.

"I have been to everybody in London who is likely to help. It is little short of a crime that the hospital should have to close down, and that's just how it stands, doesn't it, Parsons?"

The doctor nodded his head.

"I've already shut two wards out of four," he said. "We ourselves have had no salaries for a fortnight, but that, of course, does not matter. And the devil of it is that women are clamouring to get into this hospital—I've got a waiting list of nearly eighty."

Sir John nodded gravely.

"It's a terrible state of affairs," he said. "Do you know Lewinstein?"

"Slightly," said the doctor with a faint smile. "I know him well enough to cadge from him; but it was no go. Mr. Lewinstein would get no credit from having his name on our subscription list, and he is rather out for credit. As a matter of fact, he did subscribe once before. By the way, talking of Lewinstein reminds me that Lord Claythorpe, a close friend of his, has bought his niece a £50,000 pearl necklace as a wedding present. It was in all the morning papers."

"I saw it," said Sir John.

"Really, I sometimes feel that I would like to turn burglar," said the exasperated chairman, "and join the gang of that—what do you call the lady? —the person who stole that Venetian armlet that is being advertised for so industriously. She went down in the guise of a detective to Lewinstein's house. Apparently she cleared out all the guests and bolted in the night, and amongst the things she took was an armlet belonging to one of the Doges of Venice, worth a fortune. At any rate, they are advertising for its return."

"Whose is it?"

"Lord Claythorpe's. His wife was wearing it. Like a fool she took it down to Lewinstein's place. Claythorpe is a bit of a connoisseur, and they say he has been off his head since his wife came back and reported the loss."

At that moment the telephone bell rang, and the doctor pulled the instrument towards him with a little frown.

"I told those people in the office not to put anybody through," he said and lifted the receiver.

"Who's that?" he said sharply, and the soft pleasant voice of a girl replied:

"Is that Dr. Parsons?"

"Yes, it is I," said the doctor.

"Oh, I just wanted to tell you that I read your moving appeal for funds in the *Morning Post* today."

The doctor's face brightened. This little hospital was his life's work, and the very hint of a promise that help was coming, however meagre that help might be, cheered him.

"I'm glad you were moved by it," he said, half in humour and half in earnest; "and I trust that you will be moved to some purpose. Am I wrong in suspecting you to be a possible subscriber?"

There was a little laugh at the other end of the wire.

"You are appealing for £8,000 to carry on the hospital for another six months," said the girl.

"That's right," nodded the doctor.

"Well, I've sent you £10,000," was the surprising reply, and the doctor gasped.

"You've sent me £10,000!" he said hollowly. "You're joking, I suppose."

"Well, I haven't exactly sent you £10,000," said the voice—"that is to say, in money. I have sent you the money's worth. I sent a parcel to you last night. Have you got it?"

The doctor looked round.

"Yes," he said, "there is a parcel here, posted at Clapham. Is that from you?"

"That's from me," said the girl's voice. "I am relieved to know that you have found it."

"What's in it?" demanded the man curiously.

"A very interesting armlet which was, and probably is still, the property of Lord Claythorpe."

"What do you mean?" asked the doctor sharply.

"It is the armlet I stole from him," said the voice; "and there is a reward of £10,000 for its return. I want you to return it, and apply the money to your hospital."

"To whom am I speaking?" asked Dr. Parsons huskily.

"To Four Square Jane!" was the reply and there was a "click!" as the receiver was hung up.

With trembling fingers the doctor tore the tape which bound the little parcel, pulled the brown-paper cover aside, disclosing a small wooden box with a sliding lid. This he pushed back, and there, in its bed of cotton wool, glittered and flashed the famous Venetian Armlet.

It was a nine days' wonder. The daily Press, which for the past weeks had had to satisfy itself with extravagant weather reports and uninteresting divorce cases, fell upon this latest sensation with enthusiasm, and there was not a Sunday paper in the country that did not "feature" it in the largest of black type. For it was the greatest story that had been printed for years.

The securing of the reward was not to be so simple a matter as the Press and Dr. Parsons imagined. A telephone message had acquainted Lord Claythorpe with the recovery of his jewel, and the doctor himself carried it to Belgrave Square. Lord Claythorpe was a thin little man, bald of head, and yellow of face. He suffered from some sort of chronic jaundice, which not only tinged his skin, but gave a certain yellowy hue to his temper. He received the doctor in his beautiful library, one wall of which, as Dr. Parsons noticed, was covered with the doors of small safes which had been let into the wall itself. For Lord Claythorpe was a great connoisseur of precious stones, and argued that it was just as absurd to keep your gems all behind one door as it was to keep all your eggs in one basket.

"Yes, yes," he said a little testily; "that is the jewel. I wouldn't have lost it for anything. If my fool of a—if her ladyship hadn't taken it down with her I shouldn't have had all this bother and worry. This is one of the rarest ornaments in the kingdom."

He descanted upon the peculiar artistic value and historical interest of this precious armlet for the greater part of a quarter of an hour, during which time Dr. Parsons shifted uneasily from foot to foot, for no mention of the reward had been made. At last Parsons managed to murmur a hint.

"Reward—er—reward," said his lordship uncomfortably, "there was some talk of a reward. But surely, Dr. Parsons, you do not intend to benefit your—er—charitable institution at the expense of a law-abiding citizen? Or, might I say, receive a subscription at the hands of a malicious and wicked criminal?"

"I am wholly uninterested in the moral character of any person who donates money to my hospital," said Parsons boldly. "The only thing that troubles me is the lack of funds."

"Perhaps," said his lordship hopefully, "if I put my name down as an annual subscriber for——"

The doctor waited.

"Say ten guineas a year," suggested Lord Claythorpe.

"You offered a £10,000 reward," said the doctor, his anger rising. "Either your lordship is going to pay that reward or you are not. If you refuse to pay I shall go to the Press and tell them."

"The reward was for the conviction of the thief," said his lordship in triumph. "You don't deny that. Now, you haven't brought the thief along to be convicted."

"It was for any information that would lead to the recovery of the jewel," said the angry doctor; "and that is what I have brought you—not only information, but the jewel itself. There was some talk of conviction; but that, I am informed, is the usual thing to put into an advertisement of this character."

For half an hour they haggled, and the doctor was in despair. He knew that it might mean ruin to take this curmudgeon into court, and so after a painful argument he accepted, with a sense of despair, the £4,000 which Lord Claythorpe most reluctantly paid.

That night his lordship gave a dinner party in honour of his niece, whose wedding was to take place two days later. Only one person spoke at that dinner party, and that person was Lord Claythorpe. For not only had he to tell his guests what were his sensations when he learnt the jewel was lost, but he had to describe vividly and graphically his emotions on its restoration. But the choicest morsel he retained to the last.

"This doctor fellow wanted £10,000—the impertinence of it! I knew very well I was offering too large a reward, and I told those police people so. Of course, the armlet is worth three times that amount, but that is nothing to do with it. But I beat him down! I beat him down!"

"So I saw," said the easy-going Mr. Lewinstein.

"So you saw?" said Lord Claythorpe suspiciously. "Where did you see it? I thought nobody knew but myself. Has that infernal doctor been talking?"

"I expect so," said Lewinstein. "I read it in the evening papers tonight. They've got quite a story about it. I'm afraid it's not going to do you any good, Claythorpe. If Jane hears about it——"

"Jane!" scoffed his lordship. "What the deuce do I care for Jane?"

Lewinstein nodded, and catching his wife's eye, smiled.

"I didn't care for Jane—until Jane came and bit me," he said philosophically. "Until I saw her four little squares labelled on my door, and missed the contents of my private safe. I tell you that girl is no ordinary crook. She returned the armlet to you because she wanted to benefit the hospital, and if she hasn't benefited the hospital as much as she hoped I'd like to bet a thousand pounds to a penny that she's going to get the balance from you."

"Let her try!" Lord Claythorpe snapped his fingers. "For years the best burglars in Europe have been making a study of my methods, and three of them have got as far as the safe doors. But you know my system, Lewinstein," he chuckled, "ten safes, and seven of them empty. That baffles 'em! Why, Lew Smith, who is the cleverest burglar—according to Scotland Yard —who ever went into or came out of prison, worked all night on two empty safes in my cupboard."

"Doesn't anybody know which safes you use?"

"Nobody," replied the other promptly; "and only one of the three contains jewellery worth taking. No; it's nine to one against the burglar ever finding the safe."

"What do you do?" asked the interested Lewinstein. "Change the contents of the safe every night?"

Lord Claythorpe grinned and nodded.

"In the daytime," he said, "I keep most of my valuables in the big safe in the corner of my study. That is where I put such things as the Doges' armlet. At night, before the servants retire, I take all the valuable cases out of my big safe and put them on the library table. My butler and my footman stand outside the door—outside, you understand—and then I switch out all the lights, open the safe in the darkness, put in the jewellery, lock the safe, pocket my keys, and there you are!"

Lewinstein grunted, though the rest of the table had some word of applause for the genius and prescience of the little man.

"I think that's rather unnecessary," said Lewinstein, his practical mind revolting from anything which had a touch of the theatrical; "but I suppose you know your own business best."

"You suppose rightly," snapped Claythorpe, who was not used to having his judgment or his wisdom questioned.

"I can only warn you," said the persistent Lewinstein, "that in Four Square Jane you are dealing with a person who wouldn't be stopped if you had fifty safes, and a policeman sitting on top of every one of them."

"Four Square Jane!" scoffed his lordship, "don't worry about her! I have a detective here——"

Mr. Lewinstein laughed a bitter little laugh.

"So had I," he said shortly. "A female detective, may I ask?"

"Of course not. I've got the best man from Scotland Yard," said Lord Claythorpe.

"What I should like to know is this," said the other lowering his voice, "have you any kind of suspicious woman in the house?"

"What do you mean, sir?" demanded Lord Claythorpe bridling.

"Can you account for all your lady guests? There are a dozen here to-night. Do you know them all?"

"Every one of them," said his lordship promptly. "Of course, I wouldn't have strangers in the house at this moment. I have dear Joyce's wedding presents——"

"That's what I'm thinking about," said Mr. Lewinstein. "Would you mind if I had a little look round myself?"

There was a sneer on Lord Claythorpe's thin lips.

"Turning detective, Joe?" he asked.

"Something like that," said Lewinstein. "I've been bitten myself, and I know just where it hurts."

Lewinstein was given the run of the big house in Belgrave Square, and that evening he made one or two important discoveries.

The first was that "the best detective from Scotland Yard" was a private detective, and although not a Headquarters' officer, still a man of unquestionable honesty and experience, who had been employed by his lordship before.

"It's not much of a job," admitted the detective. "I have to sit with my back to the door of his study all night long. His lordship doesn't like anybody in the study itself—what's that?" he asked suddenly.

They were standing within half a dozen paces of the library door, and the detective's sensitive ears had caught a sound.

"I heard nothing," said Lewinstein.

"I swear I heard a sound inside that room. Do you mind staying here while I go for his lordship?"

"Why don't you go in?" asked the other.

"Because his lordship keeps the library door locked," grinned the detective. "I won't keep you waiting long, sir."

He found Lord Claythorpe playing bridge, and brought that nobleman along, an agitated and alarmed figure. With shaking hands he inserted the key in the lock of the heavy door and swung it open.

"You go in first, officer," he said nervously. "You'll find the switch on the right-hand side."

The room was flooded with light, but it was empty. At one end of the apartment was a long window, heavily barred. The blind was drawn, and this the detective pulled up, only to discover that the window was closed and had apparently not been opened.

"That's rum," he said. "It was the noise of a blind I heard."

"The wind?" suggested Lewinstein.

"It couldn't have been the wind, sir, the windows are hermetically closed."

"Well nobody could get in that window anyway, through the bars," said his lordship; but the detective shook his head.

"An ordinary man couldn't, sir. I'm not so sure that a young girl couldn't slip through there as easily as you slip through the door."

"Bah!" said his lordship, "you're nervous. Just take a look round, my good fellow."

There were no cupboards, and practically no places where anybody could hide, so the examination of the room was of a perfunctory character.

"Are you satisfied?" asked his lordship.

"Perfectly," said the detective, and they went out, closing the door which Lord Claythorpe locked behind them.

By half-past eleven the guests had departed, all except Lewinstein, who was hoping that he would be admitted to the curious ceremonial which Claythorpe had described. But in this he was disappointed. His lordship entered the library alone, locked the door behind him and switched out the lights, lest any prying eyes should see where he deposited the jewel cases he took from the great safe in the corner of the room. Presently they heard the soft thud of closing doors, and he emerged.

"That's all right," he said with satisfaction, as he pocketed the keys. "Now come along and have a drink before you go. You'll stay here, Johnson, won't you?" he said to the private detective.

"Yes, my lord," said the man.

On the way to the smoking-room where drinks had been served, Lord Claythorpe explained that he did not rely entirely upon the detective agency, that he had indeed notified Scotland Yard.

"The house is being watched, or will be watched, night and day until after the wedding," he said.

"I think you're wise," responded Mr. Lewinstein.

He tossed down a stiff whisky and soda, and, accompanied by his host, went into the hall where he was helped on with his coat. He was on the point of saying "Good night," when there was a thunderous knock at the front door, and the butler opened it. Two men stood on the doorstep gripping between them a frail and slender figure.

"It's all right, sir," said one, with a note of exultation, "we've got her! Can we come in?"

"Got her?" gasped his lordship, "who is it?"

And yet there was no need for him to ask.

The prisoner was a girl dressed from head to foot in black. A heavy veil covered her face, being secured apparently under the tightly-fitting little felt hat on her head.

"Caught her under your library window," said one of the men with satisfaction, and there was a grunt from Johnson the private detective.

"Who are you?" asked his lordship.

"Sergeant Felton, from Scotland Yard, sir. Are you Lord Claythorpe?"

"Yes," said his lordship.

"We've been watching the house," said the man, "and we saw her dodging down the side passage which leads to your stables. Now then, young woman, let's have a look at your face."

"No, no, no," said the girl struggling, "there are reasons. The Chief Commissioner knows the reason."

Her captor hesitated and looked at his companion.

"I think we'd better get the superintendent in charge of the case before we go any further, my lord," he said.

He took a pair of handcuffs from his pocket.

"Hold out your hands," he said, and snapped the glittering bracelets on her wrists.

"Have you got a strong room, my lord, where I can keep her till the superintendent comes?"

"In my library," said his lordship.

"Has it got a good door?"

Lord Claythorpe smiled.

He himself unlocked the library door and switched on the lights, and the girl was pushed into the room and on to a chair. The detective took a strap from his pocket and secured her ankles together.

"I'm not taking any risks with you, my lady," he said. "I don't know who you are, but I shall know in a very short time. Now I want to telephone. Have you a telephone here?"

"There is one in the hall."

The detective looked at the girl, and scratched his chin.

"I don't like leaving her alone, Robinson. You had better stay with her. Remember, you're not to take your eyes off her, see?"

They went out together, his lordship closing and locking the door behind them, whilst the man went in search of a telephone number.

"By the way, you can hear my man if he shouts, can't you?" he asked.

"No," said his lordship promptly. "You can hear nothing through that door. But surely your man is capable of looking after a girl?"

Lewinstein, a silent spectator of these happenings, smiled. He had no illusions as to the resources of that girl, and was anxious to see the end of this adventure. In the meantime, behind the locked doors of the library the girl held out her hands and the "detective" with her unlocked the handcuffs. She bent and loosened the strap, then moved quickly to the wall where the ten safes were embedded. Each she examined quickly.

"These are the three, Jimmy," she said, and her companion nodded.

"I won't ask you how you know," he said admiringly.

"It was easy," she said. "As soon as I got in here I gummed some thin black silk over the edges of each door. These three have been broken, so these three safes have been opened. We'll take a chance on this one. Give me the key."

The "detective" opened a little leather case which he had taken from his pocket, and revealed some queerly shaped instruments. Three times the girl tried, each time withdrawing the tool from the keyhole to readjust the mechanism of her skeleton key, and at the third time the lock snapped back, and the door swung open. "Got it first time," she said in triumph.

She pulled out a case, opened it and took one fleeting look, then thrust the jewel case into a long pocket on one side of her dress. In twenty seconds the safe was emptied, and the girl nodded to her companion.

"Get the window open. Put the light out first. You'll find it a squeeze, Jimmy. It's easy enough for me."

Outside the "detective-sergeant" was having trouble with the 'phone. He put it down and turned despairingly to his lordship.

"If you don't mind, sir, I'll run down to Scotland Yard. I've got a motor-bicycle waiting. I don't seem able to get into touch with the superintendent. Perhaps you wouldn't mind going into the room and keeping my man company for a little while."

"Surely," said his lordship indignantly, "your man is perfectly capable of carrying out his instructions without my assistance? I am scarcely accus-tomed——" He paused for breath.

"Very good, sir," said the "sergeant" respectfully.

A little later they heard the "pop-pop" of his motor-bicycle as it left.

"We had better do what the sergeant suggests," said Lewinstein, "we can't do any harm by going in, at any rate."

"My dear fellow," repeated his lordship testily, "that police officer is quite capable of looking after the girl. Don't you agree, Johnson?"

Johnson, the private detective, did not immediately reply.

"Well, sir," he said, "I don't mind telling you that I feel a bit uneasy about the lady being in the same room as the jewels."

"Good lord!" gasped his lordship, "I didn't think of that. Pooh! Pooh! There's a policeman with her. You know these officers, I suppose, John-son?"

"No, sir," said Mr. Johnson frankly, "I don't. I'm not brought much into touch with Scotland Yard men, and they're constantly changing from one division to another, so it's difficult to keep up with them."

His lordship pondered, a horrible fear growing within him.

"Yes, perhaps you're right, Lewinstein," he said, "we'll go in."

He put the key in the door and turned it. The room was in darkness.

"Are you there?" squeaked his lordship in such a tone of consternation that Lewinstein could have laughed.

There was a click and the lights went on, but the room was empty.

Lord Claythorpe's first glance was to the safes. Apparently they were closed, but on three of them was a square label, and Lewinstein was the first to see and understand the significance of that sign.

"What is it? What is it?" said Lord Claythorpe in a shrill tremolo, pointing with shaking fingers to the labels.

"The visiting card of Four Square Jane!" said Lewinstein.

CHAPTER 3

Chief Superintendent Dawes, of Scotland Yard, was a comparatively young man, considering the important position he held. It was the boast of his department—Peter himself did very little talking about his achievements—that never once, after he had picked up a trail, was Peter ever baffled.

A clean-shaven, youngish looking man, with grey hair at his temples, Peter took a philosophical view of crime and criminals, holding neither horror towards the former, nor malice towards the latter.

If he had a passion at all it was for the crime which contained within itself a problem. Anything out of the ordinary, or anything bizarre fascinated him, and it was one of the main regrets of his life that it had never once fallen to his lot to conduct an investigation into the many Four Square mysteries which came to the Metropolitan police.

It was after the affair at Lord Claythorpe's that Peter Dawes was turned loose to discover and apprehend this girl criminal, and he welcomed the opportunity to take charge of a case which had always interested him. To the almost hysterical telephone message Scotland Yard had received from Lord Claythorpe Peter did not pay too much attention. He realized that it was of the greatest importance that he should keep his mind unhampered and unprejudiced by the many and often contradictory "clues" which everyone who had been affected by Four Square Jane's robberies insisted on discussing with him.

He interviewed an agitated man at four o'clock in the morning, and Lord Claythorpe was frantic.

"It's terrible, terrible," he wailed, "what are you people at Scotland Yard doing that you allow these villainies to continue? It is monstrous!"

Peter Dawes, who was not unused to outbursts on the part of the victimized, listened to the squeal with equanimity.

"As I understand it, this woman came here with two men who pretended to have her in custody?"

"Two detectives!" moaned his lordship.

"If they called themselves detectives, then you were deceived," said Peter with a smile. "They persuaded you to allow the prisoner and one of her captors to spend ten minutes in the library where your jewels are kept. Now tell me, when the crime occurred had your guests left?"

Lord Claythorpe nodded wearily.

"They had all gone," he said, "except my friend Lewinstein."

Peter made an examination of the room, and a gleam of interest came into his eyes when he saw the curious labels. He examined the floor and the window-bars, and made as careful a search of the floor as possible.

"I can't do much at this hour," he said. "At daylight I will come back and have a good look through this room. Don't allow anybody in to dust or to sweep it."

He returned at nine o'clock, and to his surprise, Lord Claythorpe, whom he had expected would be in bed and asleep, was waiting for him in the library, and wearing a dressing-gown over his pyjamas.

"Look at this," exclaimed the old man, and waved a letter wildly.

Dawes took the document and read:

"You are very mean, old man! When you lost your Venetian armlet you offered a reward of ten thousand pounds. I sent that armlet to a hospital greatly in need of funds, and the doctor who presented my gift to the hospital was entitled to the full reward. I have taken your pearls because you swindled the hospital out of six thousand pounds. This time you will not get your property back."

There was no signature, but the familiar mark, roughly drawn, the four squares and the centred "J."

"This was written on a Yost," said Peter Dawes, looking at the document critically. "The paper is the common stuff you buy in penny packages—so is the envelope. How did it come?"

"It came by district messenger," said Lord Claythorpe. "Now what do you think, officer? Is there any chance of my getting those pearls back?"

"There is a chance, but it is a pretty faint one," said Peter.

He went back to Scotland Yard, and reported to his chief.

"So far as I can understand, the operations of this woman began about twelve months ago. She has been constantly robbing, not the ordinary people who are subjected to this kind of victimization, but people with bloated bank balances, and so far as my investigations go, bank balances accumulated as a direct consequence of shady exploitation companies."

"What does she do with the money?" asked the Commissioner curiously.

"That's the weird thing about it," replied Dawes. "I'm fairly certain that she donates very large sums to all kinds of charities. For example, after the Lewinstein burglary a big crèche in the East End of London received from an anonymous donor the sum of four thousand pounds. Simultaneously, another sum of four thousand was given to one of the West End hospitals. After the Talbot burglary three thousand pounds, which represented nearly the whole of the amount stolen, was left by some unknown person to the West End Maternity Hospital. I have an idea that we shall discover she is somebody who is in close touch with hospital work, and that behind these crimes there is some quixotic notion of helping the poor at the expense of the grossly rich."

"Very beautiful," said the Chief drily, "but unfortunately her admirable intentions do not interest us. In our eyes she is a common thief."

"She is something more than that," said Peter quietly; "she is the cleverest criminal that has come my way since I have been associated with Scotland Yard. This is the one thing one has dreaded, and yet one has hoped to meet—a criminal with a brain."

"Has anybody seen this woman?" said the Commissioner interested.

"They have, and they haven't," replied Peter Dawes. "That sounds cryptic, but it only means that she has been seen by people who could not recognize her again. Lewinstein saw her, Claythorpe saw her, but she was veiled and unrecognizable. My difficulty, of course, is to discover where she is going to strike next. Even if she is only hitting at the grossly rich she has forty thousand people to strike at. Obviously, it is impossible to protect them all. But somehow——" he hesitated.

"Yes?" said the Chief.

"Well, a careful study of her methods helps me a little," replied Dawes. "I have been looking round to discover who the next victim will be. He must be somebody very wealthy, and somebody who makes a parade of his wealth, and I have fined down the issue to about four men. Gregory Smith, Carl Sweiss, Mr. Thomas Scott, and John Tresser. I am inclined to believe it is Tresser she is after. You see, Tresser has made a great fortune, not by the straightest means in the world, and he hasn't forgotten to advertise his riches. He is the fellow who bought the Duke of Haslemere's house, and his collection of pictures—you will remember the stuff that has been written about."

The Chief nodded.

"There is a wonderful Romney, isn't there?"

"That's the picture," replied Dawes. "Tresser, of course, doesn't know a picture from a gas-stove. He knows that the Romney is wonderful, but only because he has been told so. Moreover, he is the fellow who has been giving the newspapers his views on charity—told them that he never spent a penny on public institutions, and never gave away a cent that he didn't get a cent's worth of value for. A thing like that would excite Jane's mind; and then, in addition, the actual artistic and monetary value of the Romney is largely advertised—why, I should imagine that the attraction is almost irresistible!"

Mr. Tresser was a difficult man to meet. His multitudinous interests in the City of London kept him busy from breakfast time until late at night. When at last Peter ran him down in a private dining-room at the Ritz-

Carlton, he found the multi-millionaire a stout, red-haired man with a long clean-shaven upper lip, and a cold blue eye.

The magic of Peter Dawes' card secured him an interview.

"Sit down—sit down," said Mr. Tresser hurriedly, "what's the trouble, hey?"

Peter explained his errand, and the other listened with interest, as to a business proposition.

"I've heard all about that Jane," said Mr. Tresser cheerfully, "but she's not going to get anything from me—you can take my word! As to the Rumney—is that how you pronounce it?—well, as to that picture, don't worry!"

"But I understand you are giving permission to the public to inspect your collection."

"That's right," said Mr. Tresser, "but everybody who sees them must sign a visitor's book, and the pictures are guarded."

"Where do you keep the Romney at night—still hanging?" asked Peter, and Mr. Tresser laughed.

"Do you think I'm a fool," he said, "no, it goes into my strong room. The Duke had a wonderful strong room which will take a bit of opening."

Peter Dawes did not share the other's confidence in the efficacy of bolts and bars. He knew that Four Square Jane was both an artist and a strategist. Of course, she might not be bothered with pictures, and, anyway, a painting would be a difficult thing to get away unless it was stolen by night, which would be hardly likely.

He went to Haslemere House, which was off Berkeley Square, a great rambling building, with a long, modern picture-gallery, and having secured admission, signed his name and showed his card to an obvious detective, he was admitted to the long gallery. There was the Romney—a beautiful example of the master's art.

Peter was the only sightseer, but it was not alone to the picture that he gave his attention. He made a brief survey of the room in case of accidents. It was long and narrow. There was only one door—that through which he had come—and the windows at both ends were not only barred, but a close wire-netting covered the bars, and made entrance and egress impossible by that way. The windows were likewise long and narrow, in keeping with the shape of the room, and there were no curtains behind which an intruder might hide. Simple spring roller blinds were employed to exclude the sunlight by day.

Peter went out, passed the men, who scrutinized him closely, and was satisfied that if Four Square Jane made a raid on Mr. Tresser's pictures, she would have all her work cut out to get away with it. He went back to Scotland Yard, busied himself in his office, and afterwards went out for lunch. He came back to his office at three o'clock, and had dismissed the matter of

Four Square Jane from his mind, when an urgent call came through. It was a message from the Assistant Chief Commissioner.

"Will you come down to my office at once, Dawes?" said the voice, and Peter sprinted down the long corridor to the bureau of the Chief Commissioner.

"Well, Dawes, you haven't had to wait long," he was greeted.

"What do you mean?" said Peter.

"I mean the precious Romney is stolen," said the Chief, and Peter could only stare at him.

"When did this happen?"

"Half an hour ago—you'd better get down to Berkeley Square, and make inquiries on the spot."

Two minutes later, Peter's little two-seater was nosing its way through the traffic, and within ten minutes he was in the hall of the big house interrogating the agitated attendants. The facts, as he discovered them, were simple.

At a quarter-past two, an old man wearing a heavy overcoat, and muffled up to the chin, came to the house, and asked permission to see the portrait gallery. He gave his name as "Thomas Smith."

He was an authority on Romney, and was inclined to be garrulous. He talked to all the attendants, and seemed prepared to give a long-winded account of his experience, his artistic training, and the excellence of his quality as an art critic—which meant that he was the type of bore that most attendants have to deal with, and they very gladly cut short his monotonous conversation, and showed him the way to the picture gallery.

"Was he alone in the room?" asked Peter.

"Yes, sir."

"And nobody went in with him?"

"No, sir."

Peter nodded.

"Of course, the garrulity may have been intentional, and it may have been designed to scare away attendants, but go on."

"The man went into the room, and was seen standing before the Romney in rapt contemplation. The attendants who saw him swore that at that time the Romney was in its frame. It hung on the level with the eyes; that is to say the top of the frame was about seven feet from the floor.

"Almost immediately after the attendants had looked in the old man came out talking to himself about the beauty of the execution. As he left the room, and came into the outer lobby, a little girl entered and also asked permission to go into the gallery. She signed her name 'Ellen Cole' in the visitors' book."

"What was she like?" said Peter.

31

"Oh, just a child," said the attendant vaguely, "a little girl."

Apparently the little girl walked into the saloon as the old man came out —he turned and looked at her, and then went on through the lobby, and out through the door. But before he got to the door, he pulled a handkerchief out of his pocket, and with it came about half a dozen silver coins, which were scattered on the marble floor of the vestibule. The attendants helped him to collect the money—he thanked them, his mind still with the picture apparently, for he was talking to himself all the time, and finally disappeared.

He had hardly left the house when the little girl came out and asked: "Which is the Romney picture?"

"In the centre of the room," they told her, "immediately facing the door."

"But there's not a picture there," she said, "there's only an empty frame, and a funny kind of little black label with four squares."

The attendants dashed into the room, and sure enough the picture had disappeared!

In the space where it had been, or rather on the wall behind the place, was the sign of Four Square Jane.

The attendants apparently did not lose their heads. One went straight to the telephone, and called up the nearest police station—the second went on in search of the old man. But all attempts to discover him proved futile. The constable on point duty at the corner of Berkeley Square had seen him get into a taxi-cab and drive away, but had not troubled to notice the number of the taxi-cab.

"And what happened to the little girl?" asked Peter.

"Oh, she just went away," said the attendant; "she was here for some time, and then she went off. Her address was in the visitor's book. There was no chance of her carrying the picture away—none whatever," said the attendant emphatically. "She was wearing a short little skirt, and light summery things, and it was impossible to have concealed a big canvas like that."

Peter went in to inspect the frame. The picture had been cut flush with the borders. He looked around, making a careful examination of the apartment, but discovered nothing, except, immediately in front of the picture, a long, white pin. It was the sort of pin that bankers use to fasten notes together. And there was no other clue.

Mr. Tresser took his loss very calmly until the newspapers came out with details of the theft. It was only then that he seemed impressed by its value, and offered a reward for its recovery.

The stolen Romney became the principal topic of conversation in clubs and in society circles. It filled columns of the newspapers, and exercised the imagination of some of the brightest young men in the amateur criminal investigation business. All the crime experts were gathered together at the scene of the happening and their theories, elaborate and ingenious, provided interesting subject matter for the speculative reader.

Peter Dawes, armed with the two addresses he had taken from the visitors' book, the address of the old man and of the girl, went round that afternoon to make a personal investigation, only to discover that neither the learned Mr. Smith nor the innocent child were known at the addresses they had given.

Peter reported to headquarters with a very definite view as to how the crime was committed.

"The old man was a blind," he said, "he was sent in to create suspicion and keep the eyes of the attendants upon himself. He purposely bored everybody with his long-winded discourse on art in order to be left alone. He went into the saloon knowing that his bulky appearance would induce the attendants to keep their eyes on him. Then he came out—the thing was timed beautifully—just as the child came in. That was the lovely plan.

"The money was dropped to direct all attention on the old man, and at that moment, probably, the picture was cut from its frame, and it was hidden. Where it was hidden, or how the girl got it out is a mystery. The attendants are most certain that she could not have had it concealed about her, and I have made experiments with a thick canvas cut to the size of the picture, and it certainly does seem that the picture would have so bulged that they could not have failed to have noticed it."

"But who was the girl?"

"Four Square Jane!" said Peter promptly.

"Impossible!"

Peter smiled.

"It is the easiest thing in the world for a young girl to make herself look younger. Short frocks, and hair in plaits—and there you are! Four Square Jane is something more than clever."

"One moment," said the Chief, "could she have handed it through the window to somebody else?"

Peter shook his head.

"I have thought of that," he said, "but the windows were closed and there was a wire-netting which made that method of disposal impossible. No, by some means or other she got the picture out under the noses of the attendants. Then she came out and announced innocently that she could not find the Romney picture—naturally there was a wild rush to the saloon. For three minutes no notice was being taken of the 'child'."

"Do you think one of the attendants was in collusion?"

"That is also possible," said Peter, "but every man has a record of good, steady service. They're all married men and none of them has the slightest thing against him."

"And what will she do with the picture? She can't dispose of it," protested the Chief.

"She's after the reward," said Peter with a smile, "I tell you, Chief, this thing has put me on my mettle. Somehow, I don't think I've got my hand on Jane yet, but I'm living on hopes."

"After the reward," repeated the Chief; "that's pretty substantial. But surely you are going to fix her when she hands the picture over?"

"Not on your life," replied Peter, and took out of his pocket a telegram and laid it on the table before the other. It read:

> The Romney will be returned on condition that Mr. Tresser undertakes to pay the sum of five thousand pounds to the Great Panton Street Hospital for Children. On his signing an agreement to pay this sum, the picture will be restored.
>
> Jane.

"What did Tresser say about that?"

"Tresser agrees," answered Peter, "and has sent a note to the secretary of the Great Panton Street Hospital to that effect. We are advertising the fact of his agreement very widely in the newspapers."

At three o'clock that afternoon came another telegram, addressed this time to Peter Dawes—it annoyed him to know that the girl was so well informed that she was aware of the fact that he was in charge of the case.

"I will restore the picture at eight o'clock tonight. Be in the picture gallery, and please take all precautions. Don't let me escape this time—The Four Square Jane."

The telegram was handed in at the General Post Office.

Peter Dawes neglected no precaution. He had really not the faintest hope that he would make the capture, but it would not be his fault if Four Square Jane were not put under lock and key.

A small party assembled in the gloomy hall of Mr. Tresser's own house.

Dawes and two detective officers, Mr. Tresser himself—he sucked at a big cigar and seemed the least concerned of those present—the three attendants, and a representative of the Great Panton Street Hospital were there.

"Do you think she'll come in person?" asked Tresser. "I would rather like to see that Jane. She certainly put one over on me, but I bear her no ill-will."

"I have a special force of police within call," said Peter, "and the roads are watched by detectives, but I'm afraid I can't promise you anything exciting. She's too slippery for us."

"Anyway, the messenger——" began Tresser.

Peter shook his head.

"The messenger may be a district messenger, though here again I have taken precautions—all the district messenger offices have been warned to notify Scotland Yard in the event of somebody coming with a parcel addressed here."

Eight o'clock boomed out from the neighbouring church, but Four Square Jane had not put in an appearance. Five minutes later there came a ring at the bell, and Peter Dawes opened the door.

It was a telegraph boy.

Peter took the buff envelope and tore it open, read the message through carefully, and laughed—a hopeless, admiring laugh.

"She's done it," he said.

"What do you mean?" asked Tresser.

"Come in here," said Peter.

He led the way into the picture gallery. There was the empty frame on the wall, and behind it the half-obliterated label which Four Square Jane had stuck.

He walked straight to the end of the room to one of the windows.

"The picture is here," he said, "it has never left the room."

He lifted his hand, and pulled at the blind cord, and the blind slowly revolved.

There was a gasp of astonishment from the gathering. For, pinned to the blind, and rolled up with it, was the missing Romney.

* * * *

"I ought to have guessed when I saw the pin," said Peter to his chief. It was quick work, but it was possible to do it.

"She cut out the picture, brought it to the end of the room, and pulled down the blind; pinned the top corners of the picture to the blind, and let it roll up again. Nobody thought of pulling that infernal thing down!"

"The question that worries me," said the Chief, "is this—Who *is* Four Square Jane?"

"That," replied Peter, "is just what I am going to discover."

CHAPTER 4

Mrs. Gordon Wilberforce was a large, yielding lady of handsome and aristocratic features and snow-white hair. It is true that she had not reached the age when one expected hair of that snowy whiteness, and there were people who told with brutal frankness a story that was not creditable to Mrs. Wilberforce.

According to these gossips the lady had attended the salon of a famous beauty doctor, who had endeavoured to restore Mrs. Wilberforce's hair to the beautiful golden hue which was so attractive to her friends and admirers in the late eighties. But the beauty doctor had not had that success which his discreet advertisements seemed to guarantee. One half of Mrs. Wilberforce's hair had come out green, and the other a deep pinky russet brown. Thereupon, Mrs. Wilberforce, with great heroism, had ordered the trembling hair-dresser to bleach without mercy.

And in course of time she appeared in her family circle. She explained that her hair had gone white in a night with the worry she had had from Joyce.

Joyce Wilberforce distressed her mother for many reasons. Not the least of these was the fact that her mother did not understand her, and Joyce did understand her mother.

They sat at breakfast in their little morning-room overlooking Hyde Park, Mrs. Wilberforce and her daughter, and the elder woman was very thoughtful.

"Joyce," she said, "pay attention to what I am going to say, and try to keep your mind from wandering."

"Yes, mother," said the girl meekly.

"Do you remember that maid we discharged, Jane Briglow?"

"Jane Briglow?" said the girl, "yes, I remember her very well. You didn't like her manner or something."

"She gave herself airs," said Mrs. Wilberforce tartly.

The girl's lips curved in a smile. Joyce and her mother were never wholly in harmony. It was not the first time they had discussed Jane Briglow in the same spirit of antagonism which marked their present conversation.

"Jane was a good girl," said Joyce quietly. "She was a little romantic, rather fond of sensational literature, but there was nothing wrong with her."

Mrs. Wilberforce sniffed.

"I am glad you think so," she said, and the girl looked up quickly.

"Why do you say that, mother?"

"Well," said Mrs. Wilberforce," doesn't it seem strange to you that this horrible burglar person should also be called Jane?"

Joyce laughed.

"It is not an uncommon name," she said.

"But she is going about her work in an uncommon manner," said her mother. "All the people she is robbing are personal friends of ours, or of dear Lord Claythorpe. I must say," she went on with a little shiver of exasperation, "that you take your loss very well. I suppose you realize that a £50,000 necklace intended for you has disappeared?"

Joyce nodded.

"Purchased to deck the sacrifice," she said ironically.

"Rubbish!" snorted Mrs. Wilberforce, "sacrifice indeed! You are marrying Lord Claythorpe's heir, and Lord Claythorpe was your uncle's dearest friend."

"He is not my dearest friend," said the girl grimly in a sudden fit of exasperation. "Because one's been brought up with a person, regarding him almost as a brother, that is no reason why one should marry him. In fact to the contrary. No one has yet accused me of being weak, but I should certainly lose all my self-respect if I allowed myself to be married off in this way."

"It seems to me," said Mrs. Wilberforce, "that for a girl who has no other prospects of marriage, you are arguing with great passion. And short-sightedness," she added.

"It isn't a question of wanting to marry someone else," said Joyce, after a perceptible pause, "it's merely a question of not wanting to marry Francis."

She walked across the room and picked up a silver-framed photograph of the young man under discussion.

"And I think I'm justified," she concluded.

Mrs. Wilberforce was silent.

"After all, why shouldn't I marry whom I choose," said Joyce. "Don't you realize that Lord Claythorpe is being horribly selfish and that this marriage is being designed for his own purpose?"

"I realize one thing," said Mrs. Wilberforce angrily, "and that is that you look like being pig-headed enough to ruin your own chances socially, and both of us financially. You know as well as I do, Joyce, that Lord

Claythorpe is acting absolutely in accordance with your uncle's will, and you cannot doubt that your uncle had your best interests at heart."

"When uncle left his great fortune to me and made the provision that I should not marry anybody who was not the choice of Lord Claythorpe, the trustee of his estate, the poor dear old man thought he was protecting my interests, because he had a most childlike faith in Lord Claythorpe's honesty. He never dreamt that Lord Claythorpe would choose his own idiot son!"

"Idiot!" gasped Mrs. Wilberforce, "that is an outrageous statement. He's not one of the intellectuals, perhaps, but he's a good boy, and one day will become Lord Claythorpe."

"So far as I can see," said the girl, "that's his only virtue. You can turn the matter about as you like, mother, but there the fact remains. Unless I marry Francis Claythorpe I lose a great fortune. Lord Claythorpe can well afford to give me £50,000 necklaces!"

Mrs. Wilberforce smoothed her dress over her knees patiently.

"The provision was a very wise one, my dear," she said, "otherwise you would have married that awful person Jamieson Steele. Imagine, a penniless engineer and a forger!"

The girl sprang to her feet, her face crimson.

"You shall not say that, mother," she said sharply. "Jamieson did not forge Lord Claythorpe's signature. The cheque which was presented and paid to Jamieson was signed by Lord Claythorpe, and if he repudiated his own signature he did it for his own purpose. He knew I was fond of Jamieson. It was cruel, terribly cruel!"

Mrs. Wilberforce raised her hands in protest.

"Do not let us have a scene," she said, "my dear girl, think of all your money means to me. The years I've scrimped and saved to get you an education and put you in a position in society. Perhaps Jamieson was led astray _____"

"I tell you he did *not* do it," cried the girl. "The charge against him was made by Lord Claythorpe in order to discredit him and give him a reason for refusing his consent to our marriage."

Mrs. Wilberforce shrugged her ample shoulders.

"Well, there's no sense in going into the question now," she said, "let us forget all about it. Jamieson has disappeared, and I hope he is living a virtuous life in the Colonies."

The girl shrugged her shoulders. She knew it was useless to continue any argument with her mother. She changed the subject.

"What is this about Jane Briglow?" she asked. "Have you seen her?"

Mrs. Wilberforce shook her head.

"No," she said, "but in the night I have been thinking things out, and I have decided that Jane knows something about these crimes. From all the descriptions I have had of this girl I can reach no other conclusion than that she has something to do with the burglaries."

The girl laughed.

"Don't you think Jamieson may also have had something to do with them?" she asked satirically, and Mrs. Wilberforce tightened her lips.

"You have a very bitter tongue, Joyce; I am rather sorry for poor Francis."

The girl rose and walked across to the window, staring out across the park, and Mrs. Wilberforce eyed her anxiously.

"You are a queer girl, Joyce," she said, "you are going to be married tomorrow, and tomorrow you will be a rich woman in your own right. One might imagine that you were going to be hanged."

A maid came in at this moment.

"Lord Claythorpe and Mr. Claythorpe," she announced, and Mrs. Wilberforce arose with a beaming face.

The youth who followed his lordship into the room was tall and lank. A small weak face on an absurdly small head, round shoulders, long and awkward arms—if Joyce did not look like a bride in prospective, this young man certainly had no appearance of being a bridegroom of the morrow.

He gave Mrs. Wilberforce a limp hand and shuffled across to the girl.

"I say," he said in a high-pitched voice, which ended in a little giggle, "awfully bad luck about losing those pearls, what?"

The girl looked at him thoughtfully.

"How do you feel about getting married, Francis?" she asked.

He shrugged his shoulders.

"Oh, I don't know," he said vaguely; "it really doesn't make much difference to me. Of course, I shall have to explain to quite a lot of people, and there'll be a lot of heartaches and all that sort of thing."

She could have laughed, but she kept a straight face.

"Yes, I suppose I have disappointed a number of very charming friends of yours," she said drily, "still, they can't all have this paragon."

"That's what I say," said Mr. Claythorpe, and then giggled again, his hand straying to his pocket.

This young man had no small opinion of his own powers of fascination, and was, by his own standards, something of a Lothario.

"What's so jolly amusing," he said with a little snigger, "is that not only the people one knows are upset, but quite a lot of unknown people. People, or girls I have quite forgotten are terribly distressed about it. You don't mind if I show you a letter?" he asked mysteriously.

She shook her head.

He took an ornamental case from his pocket, opened it, and produced a heavily scented letter.

He unfolded the thick sheet of note-paper, and read:—

"I have only just read the terrible news that you are being married to-morrow. Won't you see me once, just once, for the sake of the happy day long ago? I must see you before you are married. I must take farewell of you in person. Believe me, I will never trouble you again. You used to praise my pretty face; won't you see it again for the last time? If you will, put an 'agony' advertisement in *The Times*, and I will meet you at the Albert Gate, Regents Park, at nine o'clock tomorrow night."

"That's tonight," explained the young man.

"Who is she?" asked the girl curiously.

"The Lord knows!" said Mr. Claythorpe with a cheerful smirk; "of course, dear old thing, I'll have to see her. I put the advertisement in. You're sure you don't mind?"

She shook her head.

"I haven't told the governor," said the young man, "and I want you to keep it dark. You see he's a bit old-fashioned in things like that, and he hasn't got your broad outlook, Joyce. And for heaven's sake, don't breathe a word to Father Maggerley; you know what a stick he is!"

"Father Maggerley," repeated the girl, "oh, yes, we're lunching with him, aren't we?"

"Personally," the young man babbled on, "I think it's a little indecent for a bride and bridegroom to lunch with the fellow who's going to tie them up. But the governor's frightfully keen on Maggerley. He's even dining with us tonight, as well. I hope he doesn't give me any good advice, or I shall have a few words to say to him."

He braced his lean shoulders with a determined air, and again the girl had to suppress a smile.

She went up to her room soon after, and did not appear until the car had arrived at the door to carry them to Ciro's. Father Maggerley, who was the fifth member of the party, was a tall aesthetic man, reputed to be very "high church," and suspected of leanings towards the papacy.

It was not remarkable that the conversation turned upon Four Square Jane. It was a subject in which Lord Claythorpe was tremendously interested, and as he listened to Mrs. Wilberforce's theories, his lined yellow face betrayed signs of unusual alertness.

"The police will have her sooner or later," he said viciously, "you can be sure of that."

Francis was bubbling over with good humour. The girl had interrupted him in the morning at the point when he was telling her news, which was no news at all, since he had imparted the information, not once but a dozen times in the course of the past week, that he carried in his pocket the wedding ring which was to unite them. He took it out and showed it to her, a thin circle of shining platinum, but Joyce was not enthusiastic over its beauties, and after a long exposition of his own good taste in jewellery, Francis rambled on to another and equally uninteresting subject.

For all that, the lunch was not without interest to Joyce. For again and again the conversation returned to Four Square Jane, and, as Joyce had admitted to her mother that morning, she had a certain sympathy with this criminal because her activities had been directed towards people who were particularly loathsome from Joyce's own point of view.

That night the amorous Francis set forth in a spirit of high adventure to meet his unknown adorer. He came to his father's dinner table late, in a tremble of excitement, and blurted forth his version of the meeting.

"Do you mean to say you didn't know her?" asked Lord Claythorpe disapprovingly.

"No, sir," said the young man. "I couldn't see her face. She was veiled. She was sitting in a car, and beckoned me from the side-walk. I got in and had a little chat with her, and then"—with a fine air of unconcern—"she just put her arms round my neck, held me tight for a second, and then said, 'I can stand no more, Francis; go.'"

"Very singular," said the Reverend Mr. Maggerley thoughtfully, "very singular indeed. Poor soul, possibly she will now seek a life of seclusion in one of our religious houses."

"It was a stupid thing to do," rapped Lord Claythorpe, "meeting a person you didn't know. I am surprised at you, Francis, on your wedding eve."

Mr. Maggerley was probably more impressed by the incident than his patron. As he walked home that night, to his house in Kensington, he evolved a sermon from the incident—a sermon which could not fail to gain a measure of comment from the lay press. He reached his austere dwelling, and was received by a butler of solemn and respectful mien.

"Sister Agatha is waiting for you in the study, sir," he said in a low voice.

"Sister Agatha?" repeated Mr. Maggerley. "I don't remember Sister Agatha."

This was not remarkable, for there were many sisters attached to the various Orders in which Father Maggerley was interested, and it was impossible that he should remember their names.

He went up to his study wondering what urgent business could bring a sister of charity to his house at this hour. The light was burning in the study, but Sister Agatha was not there. He summoned the butler, and that gentleman was frankly nonplussed.

"It's very extraordinary, sir, but I showed the sister in here, and I've been in the hall, or in view of the hall ever since."

"Well, she's not here now," said Father Maggerley humorously. "I'm afraid, Jenkins, you've been sleeping."

A thought occurred to him, an alarming thought, and he made a rapid inspection of the study. He was relieved to find that not so much as a newspaper had been moved, that his priceless Venetian glasses were untouched, so he dismissed Sister Agatha from his mind and went to bed.

The marriage of Mr. Francis Claythorpe and Miss Joyce Wilberforce was one of the social events of the season. The big porch of St. Giles was crowded with a fashionable congregation. The girl, looking paler than usual, came to the church with her mother, and was received by an uncomfortable-looking bridegroom and by Lord Claythorpe, who did not disguise his good cheer and satisfaction. Today represented to him the culmination of a long-planned scheme. Not even the grey envelope which was in his pocket, and which he had found on his breakfast table that morning, distressed him, although it bore the curious signature of Four Square Jane. The letter read:—

"You are very mean, Lord Claythorpe. Today, by sacrificing the happiness of a young girl, you are endeavouring to bring riches to your almost bankrupt estate. You have betrayed the trust of one who had faith in you and have utilised the provisions of his foolish will in order to enrich your family. There is many a slip between the cup and the lip."

"Pooh!" said Lord Claythorpe on reading this. "Pooh!" he said again, and his son looked up over his cup and asked for an explanation. That explanation Lord Claythorpe peremptorily refused.

* * * *

Francis Claythorpe moved forward to meet the girl and, contrary to the usual custom, walked up the aisle with her, and took his place at the altar rails. As he did so, the Reverend Father Maggerley entered from the side door and paced slowly to the centre of the church.

"The ring, Francis?" muttered Lord Claythorpe in his son's ear, and Francis took a little case from his pocket with a satisfied grin.

He opened it and gasped.

"It's gone!" he said in so loud a voice that everyone in the neighbouring pews could hear.

Lord Claythorpe did not curse, but he said something very forcibly. It was Mrs. Wilberforce whose presence of mind saved a situation which might otherwise have proved rather embarrassing. She slipped her own wedding-ring off, and passed it to the young man, and the girl watched the proceedings with a smile of indifference.

As young Lord Claythorpe fumbled with the ring the vestry door opened and someone beckoned to the clergyman. The Reverend Father Maggerley, with a little frown at this indecorous interruption, paced back to the door in his stately fashion and disappeared. He was gone some time, and there was a little murmur of wonder in the congregation when he reappeared and called Lord Claythorpe towards him.

And then to the amazement of the congregation, the whole wedding party disappeared into the vestry. It was a queer situation which met them. On the table of the vestry lay a long envelope inscribed—"Marriage Licence of the Honourable Francis Claythorpe and Miss Joyce Wilberforce."

"I am exceedingly sorry," said Mr. Maggerley in a troubled voice, as he picked up the envelope, "but something unaccountable has happened."

"What is it?" said Claythorpe sharply.

"This license," began the clergyman.

"Yes, yes," snapped Claythorpe, "I gave it to you the day before yesterday. It is a special license—there's nothing wrong with it, is there?"

Mr. Maggerley could not answer immediately.

"It was in my safe, in my own study," he said, "I can't understand it. Nobody has access to the safe but myself, and yet——"

"And yet what?" wailed Mrs. Wilberforce. "Tell me, for heavens' sake, what has happened?"

For answer, Father Maggerley took a slip of paper from the envelope, opened it and handed it without a word to Lord Claythorpe.

"That is all it contains," said the clergyman, and Claythorpe swore under his breath, for instead of the license were the four familiar squares.

"Four Square Jane!" he muttered. "How did she get this?"

Mr. Maggerley shook his head.

"I can't understand," he began, and then he remembered Sister Agatha. Sister Agatha, who had arrived unexpectedly, who had remained in his study for the greater part of an hour, and had disappeared unseen by anybody.

So Sister Agatha had been Four Square Jane!

CHAPTER 5

Peter Dawes, of Scotland Yard, and a very gloomy Lord Claythorpe sat in conference in the latter gentleman's City office. For Lord Claythorpe was a director of many companies, and had interests of a wide and varied character.

The detective sat at a table, with a little block of paper before him, jotting down notes from time to time, and there was a frown upon his face which suggested that his investigations were not going exactly as he could have wished them.

"There is the case," said Lord Claythorpe. "The whole thing was a malicious act on the part of this wretched woman, directed against me, my son, and my niece."

"Is Miss Joyce Wilberforce your niece?" asked the detective, and Lord Claythorpe hesitated.

"Well, she is not my niece," he said at last. "Rather she was the niece of one of my dearest friends. He was an immensely wealthy man, and when he died he left the bulk of his property to his niece."

The detective nodded.

"Where does your interest come in, Lord Claythorpe?" he asked.

"I am her legal guardian," said his lordship, "although of course, she has a mother. That is to say, I am the trustee and sole executor of her estate, and there were one or two provisions especially made by my dear friend which gave me authority usually denied to trustees——"

"Such as the right of choosing her husband," said the detective quietly, and it was Lord Claythorpe's turn to frown.

"So you know something about this, do you?" he asked. "Yes, I have that right. It so happened that I chose my own son Francis as the best man for that position, and the lady was quite agreeable."

"Indeed!" said the polite Peter. He consulted his notes. "As far as I understand, this mysterious person, whom Mrs. Wilberforce believes to be a discharged employee named Jane Briglow, after making several raids upon your property, reached the culmination of her audacity by robbing your son of his wedding-ring and then burgling the house of the parson who was to marry them and stealing the license, which had been granted by the Bishop of London."

"That's it exactly," said Lord Claythorpe.

"And what of the wedding?" asked Peter. "There will be no difficulty of getting another license."

Lord Claythorpe sniffed.

"The only difficulty is," he said, "that the young lady is naturally prostrated by the humiliation which this villainous woman has thrust upon her. She was in such a state of collapse the following morning that her mother was compelled to take her—or rather, to send her—to a friend in the country. The wedding is postponed for, let us say, a month."

"One other question," asked the detective. "You say you suspect, in addition to Jane Briglow, a young man named Jamieson Steele, who was in a way engaged to Miss Joyce Wilberforce?"

"A fugitive from justice," said his lordship emphatically. "And why you police fellows cannot catch him is beyond my understanding. The man forged my name——"

"I know all about that," said the detective. "I had the records of the case looked out, and the particulars of the case were 'phoned to me here whilst you had gone upstairs to collect data concerning the previous robbery. As a matter of fact, although he is, as you may say, a fugitive from justice, having very foolishly run away, there is no evidence which would secure a conviction before a judge and jury. I suppose your lordship knows that?"

His lordship did not know that, and he expressed his annoyance in the usual manner—which was to abuse the police.

Peter Dawes went back to Scotland Yard, and consulted the officer who had been in charge of the forgery case.

"No, sir," said that individual, "we have not a picture of Mr. Steele. But he was a quiet enough young fellow—a civil engineer, so far as my memory serves me, in the employment of one of Lord Claythorpe's companies."

Peter Dawson looked at the other thoughtfully. His informant was Chief Inspector Passmore, who was a living encyclopædia, not only upon the aristocratic underworld, but upon crooks who moved in the odour of respectability.

"Inspector," said Peter, "what position does Lord Claythorpe occupy in the world of the idle rich?"

The inspector stroked his stubbly chin.

"He is neither idle nor rich," he said. "Claythorpe is, in point of fact, a comparatively poor man, most of whose income is derived from directors' fees. He has been a heavy gambler in the past, and only as recently as the last oil slump he lost a goodish bit of money."

"Married?" asked Peter, and the other nodded.

"To a perfectly colourless woman whom nobody seems to have met, though I believe she is seen out at some of the parties Lewinstein gives," he said.

"Do you know anything about the fortune of Miss Joyce Wilberforce?"

"Two hundred and fifty thousand pounds," said the other promptly. "Held absolutely by his lordship as sole trustee. The girl's uncle thought an awful lot of him, and my own opinion is that, in entrusting the girl's fortune to Claythorpe, he was a trifle mad."

The men's eyes met.

"Is Claythorpe crooked?" asked Dawes bluntly, and the detective shrugged his shoulders.

"Heaven knows," he said. "The only thing I am satisfied about is his association with Four Square Jane."

Peter looked at him with a startled gaze.

"What on earth do you mean?" he asked.

"Well," said the inspector, "don't you see how all these crimes which are committed by Four Square Jane have as their object the impoverishment of Claythorpe?"

"I have formed my own theory on that," said Peter slowly. "I thought Four Square Jane was a society crook doing a Claude Duval stunt, robbing the rich to keep the poor."

The inspector smiled.

"You got that idea from the fact that she gives the proceeds of her jewel robberies to the hospitals. And why shouldn't she? They're difficult to dispose of, and as a rule they're easily retrievable if old man Claythorpe will pay the price. But you never heard, when she took solid money, that that went to hospitals, did you?"

"There have been instances," said Peter.

"When it wasn't Claythorpe's money," said the other quickly. "When it was only the money belonging to some pal of Claythorpe's as shady as himself. The impression I get of Four Square Jane is that she's searching for something all the time. Maybe it's money—at any rate, when she gets money she sticks to it; and maybe it's something else."

"What is your theory?" asked Dawes.

"My theory," said the inspector slowly, "is that Four Square Jane and Claythorpe were working in a crooked game together, and that he double-crossed her and that she is getting her revenge."

* * * *

Lord Claythorpe had his office in the City, but most of his business was conducted in a much smaller office situated in St. James' Street. The sole staff of this bureau was his confidential clerk, Donald Remington, a sour-faced man of fifty, reticent and taciturn, who knew a great deal more about his lordship's business than possibly even Lord Claythorpe gave him credit for.

After his interview with the detective, Lord Claythorpe drove away from the city to the West End, and went up the one flight of stairs which led to the little suite—it was more like a flat than an office and occupied the first floor of a shop building, being approached by the side door—in an absent and abstracted frame of mind.

The silent Remington rose as his master entered, and Lord Claythorpe took the seat which his subordinate had occupied. For fully three minutes neither man spoke, and then Remington asked:

"What did the detective want your lordship for?"

"To ask about that infernal woman," replied the other shortly.

"Four Square Jane, eh? But did he ask you anything else?" His tone was one of respectful familiarity, if the paradox may be allowed.

Claythorpe nodded.

"He wanted to know about Miss Wilberforce's fortune," he said.

Another silence, and then Remington asked:

"I suppose you'll be glad when that wedding is through, now?"

There was a significant note in his voice, and Claythorpe looked up.

"Of course, I shall," he said sharply. "By the way, have you made arrangements about——"

Remington nodded.

"Do you think you're wise?" he asked. "The securities had better stay in the vaults at the bank don't you think, especially in view of this girl's activities?"

"Nothing of the sort," replied Claythorpe violently. "Carry out my instructions, Remington, to the letter. What the devil do you mean by questioning any act of mine?"

Remington raised his eyebrows the fraction of an inch.

"Far be it from me to question your lordship's actions; I am merely suggesting that——"

"Well, suggest nothing," said Lord Claythorpe. "You have given notice to the bank that I intend putting the bonds in a place of security?"

"I have," replied the other, "the manager has arranged for the box to be delivered here this afternoon. The assistant manager and the accountant are bringing it."

"Good!" said Claythorpe, "tomorrow I will take it down to my country place."

Remington was silent.

"You don't think it wise, eh?" the small eyes of Lord Claythorpe twinkled with malicious humour. "I see you're scared of Four Square Jane, too."

"Not I," said Remington quickly. "When is this marriage to occur?"

"In a month," said his lordship airily. "I suppose you're thinking about your bonus."

Remington licked his dry lips.

"I am thinking about the sum of four thousand pounds which your lordship owes me, and which I have been waiting for very patiently for the last two years," he said. "I am tired of this kind of work, and I am anxious to have a little rest and recreation. I'm getting on in years, and it's very nearly time I had a change."

Lord Claythorpe was scribbling idly on his blotting-pad.

"How much do you think I will owe you, altogether, with the bonus I promised you for your assistance?"

"Nearer ten thousand pounds than four," replied the man.

"Oh!" said his lordship carelessly. "That is a large sum, but you may depend upon receiving it the moment my boy is married. I have been spending a lot of money lately, Remington. It cost a lot to get back that pearl necklace."

"You mean the Venetian Armlet?" said the other quickly. "I didn't know that you had the pearl necklace back?"

"Anyway, I advertised for it," said his lordship evasively.

"Fixing no definite reward," said Remington, "and for a very good reason."

"What do you mean?" asked Lord Claythorpe quickly.

"The pearls were faked," said the calm Remington. "Your fifty thousand pound necklace was worth little more than fifty pounds!"

"Hush! for heavens' sake," said Claythorpe. "Don't talk so loud." He mopped his brow. "You seem to know a devil of a lot," he said suspiciously. "In fact, there are moments, Remington, when I think you know a damn sight too much for my comfort."

Remington smiled for the first time—a thin hard smile that gave his face a sinister appearance.

"All the more reason why your lordship should get rid of me as soon as possible," he said. "I have no ambition except to own a little cottage in Cornwall, where I can fish, ride a horse, and idle away my time."

His lordship rose hurriedly and took off his coat, preparatory to washing his hands in a small wash-place leading from the office.

"It's getting late," he said. "I had forgotten I have to lunch with somebody. Your ambition shall be gratified—be sure of that, Remington," he said, passing into the smaller room.

"I hope so," said Remington. His eyes were fixed on the floor. In throwing down his coat a letter had dropped from Claythorpe's pocket, and Remington stooped to pick it up. He saw the postmark and the handwriting, and recognized it as that of Mrs. Wilberforce. He heard the splash of the water in the bowl and lord Claythorpe's voice humming a little tune. Without a moment's hesitation he took it out and read it. The letter was short.

"My dear Lord Claythorpe," it ran. "Joyce is adamant on the point of the marriage, and says she will not go through with it for another twelve months."

He replaced the letter in the envelope, and put it back in the inside pocket of the coat.

Twelve months! Claythorpe had lied when he said a month, and was obviously lying with a purpose.

When his lordship emerged, wiping his hands on a towel, and still humming a little tune, Remington was gazing out of the window upon the chimney tops of Jermyn Street.

"I shall be back at half-past two," said Lord Claythorpe, perfunctorily examining a small heap of letters which lay on his desk. "The bank people will be here by then?"

Remington nodded.

"I am worried about this transfer of Miss Joyce's securities," he said. "They are safe enough in the bank. I do not think they will be safe with you."

"Rubbish," said his lordship. "I think I know how to deal with Four Square Jane. And besides, I am going to ensure the safety of the securities. Four Square Jane isn't the kind of person who would steal paper security. It wouldn't be any good to her, anyway."

"But suppose these documents disappear?" persisted Remington. "Though it might not assist Four Square Jane, it would considerably embarrass you and Miss Joyce. It would not be a gain, perhaps, to the burglar, but it would be a distinct loss to the young lady."

"Don't worry," said Claythorpe, "neither Four Square Jane nor her confederate, Mr. Jamieson Steele—"

"Jamieson Steele?" repeated Remington. "What has he to do with it?"

Lord Claythorpe chuckled.

"It is my theory—and it is a theory, I think, which is also held by the police—that Jamieson Steele is the gentleman who assists Miss Four Square Jane in her robberies."

"I'll never believe it," said Remington.

Lord Claythorpe had his hand on the door, preparatory to departing, and he turned at these words.

"Perhaps you do not believe that he forged my name to a cheque in this very office?" he said.

"I certainly do not believe that," said Remington. "In fact I know that that story is a lie."

Claythorpe's face went red.

"That is an ugly word to use to me, Remington," he said, "I think the sooner you go the better."

"I quite agree with your lordship," said Remington, and smiled as the door slammed behind his irate master.

When Claythorpe returned he was in a more amicable frame of mind, and greeted the two bank officials with geniality. On the big table was a black japanned box, heavily sealed. The business of transferring the sealed packages which constituted the contents of the box was not a long process. Lord Claythorpe checked them with a list he took from his case, and signed a receipt.

"I suppose your lordship would not like to break the seals of these envelopes?" said the assistant bank manager. "Of course, we are not responsible for their contents, but it would be more satisfactory to us, as I am sure it would be to your lordship, if you were able to verify the contents."

"It is not necessary," said Claythorpe, with a wave of his hand. "I'll just reseal the box and put it in my safe."

This he did in the presence of the manager, locking away the box in an old-fashioned steel safe—a proceeding which the bankers witnessed without enthusiasm.

"That doesn't seem very secure," said one, "I wish your lordship——"

"I wish you would mind your own business," said Lord Claythorpe, and the bankers left, "blessing" the truculent man under their breath.

At six o'clock that afternoon Claythorpe finished the work on which he had been engaged, closed and locked his desk, tried the safe, and put on his hat. He glanced through the front window and saw that his car was waiting, and that it was pelting with rain.

"Which way are you going, Remington?" he asked. "I can give you a lift as far as Park Lane."

"No, thank you, my lord," said Remington, struggling into his mackintosh. "I am going by tube, and I have not far to walk."

They went out of the office together, double-locking the stout door. Before leaving, Remington attached a burglar alarm which communicated with a large bell outside the building, and he repeated this process before the door was actually closed and double-locked.

"I want you to be here at nine o'clock tomorrow morning," said Claythorpe to his subordinate. "Good-night."

The inclemency of the weather increased as the evening advanced. A howling south-west gale swept over London, clearing the streets of idlers and limiting to some extent the activities of the police patrols. The police officer who was on duty within a few yards of the building, and who was relieved at eleven o'clock that night, stated that he saw or heard nothing of a suspicious character. In the course of his tour of duty, he tried the door which led to Lord Claythorpe's office but found it fastened. His relief, a man named Tomms, made an examination of the door at a quarter past eleven—it was his business to examine every door in the street to see that they were securely fastened—and, in addition, acting upon instructions received from Scotland Yard, "pegged" the door. That is to say, he inserted two small wedges of the size of match sticks, one in each door-post, and tied a piece of black cotton from one to the other.

At one o'clock he tried the door again, and flashed his lamp upon the black thread, and found that it had been broken. This could only mean that someone had passed into the office between eleven and one. He summoned assistance, and roused the caretaker, who lived in adjoining premises, and together they went into the darkened building, and mounted the stairs.

Lord Claythorpe's office door was apparently closed. It led, as the caretaker explained, directly into the main office. There was no sign of jemmy work, and the officers might have given up their investigations and found a simple explanation for the broken thread in the wildness of the night, when, flashing his lamp on the floor, one of the policemen saw a thin trickle of red coming from beneath. It was blood!

The police did not hesitate, but smashed open the door, and entered with some difficulty, for immediately behind the door was lying the body of a man. Tomms switched on the light and knelt down by the side of the body.

"He's dead," he said. "Do you know this man?"

"Yes, sir," said the white-faced caretaker, "that's Mr. Remington."

The police made a perfunctory examination.

"You'd better get the divisional surgeon, Jim," he said to his comrade. "But I'm afraid it's no use. This poor fellow has been shot through the heart."

He looked round the apartment. The safe door was wide open and empty.

Half-an-hour later Peter Dawes arrived on the scene of the murder and made a brief examination. He looked at the body.

"Was he like this?" he asked, "when you found him?"

"Yes, sir," replied the officer.

"He has a knife in his hand."

Peter bent down and looked at the thin-bladed weapon, tightly clenched in the dead man's hand.

"What's that, sir?" said Tomms, pointing to the other hand. "It looks like a paper there."

The card in Remington's half-clenched fist was loosely held, and the detective gently withdrew it. It was a visiting-card, and the name inscribed thereon was, "Mr. Jamieson Steele, Civil Engineer." Peter Dawes whistled, and then walked across to the safe.

"That's queer," he said, and swung the door of the safe closed in the hope of finding something behind it.

He found something, but not what he had expected. In the centre of the green steel door was a small label. It was a label bearing the mark of Four Square Jane.

CHAPTER 6

Four Square Jane had committed a murder! It was incredible. All Peter Dawes' fine theories went by the board in that discovery. This was not the work of a society crook; it was not the work of a criminal philanthropist; there was evidence here of the most cold-blooded murder that it had been his business to investigate.

Summoned from his bed at three o'clock in the morning, Lord Claythorpe came to his office a greatly distressed man. He was shivering from sheer terror when he told the story of the securities which had been in the safe when he had left the office.

"And I was warned. I was warned!" he cried. "Poor Remington himself begged me not to do it. What a fool I am!"

"What was Remington doing here?" asked Peter.

The body of the murdered man had long since been removed to the mortuary, and only the dark stain on the floor spoke eloquently of tragedy.

"I haven't any idea," said his lordship. "I simply dare not let myself think. Poor fellow! It is a tragedy, an appalling tragedy!"

"I know all about that," said Peter drily. "Murders usually are. But what was Remington doing in this office between eleven at night and one o'clock in the morning?"

Lord Claythorpe shook his head.

"I can only offer you my theory," he said, "for what it is worth. Poor Remington was greatly worried about the securities being in this office at all, and he begged me to get a caretaker, a commissionaire or somebody, to sit in the office during the night. Very foolishly I rejected this excellent suggestion. I can only surmise that, worried by the knowledge that so many valuable securities were in this inadequate safe, Remington came in the middle of the night, intending to remain on guard himself."

Peter nodded. It was a theory which had the appearance of being a feasible one.

"Then you think that he was surprised by the burglar?"

"Or burglars," said Lord Claythorpe. "Yes, I do."

Peter sat at his lordship's desk, tapping at the blotting-pad with his fingers.

"There is a lot to support your theory," he said. "From the appearance of the body and the weapon in his hand, it is a likely suggestion that he was defending himself. On the other hand, look at this."

He took a crumpled envelope from his pocket and laid it on the table. It was stained with blood and the flap was heavily sealed.

"We found this under his body," said the detective. "You will note that the envelope has been slit open by some sharp instrument—in fact, such an instrument as was found in Remington's hand when the body was discovered."

His lordship pondered this.

"Possibly he surprised them in the act of opening the envelope, and snatched it away," he said, and again the detective nodded.

"I agree with you that that is also a plausible theory," he said. "Had he a key of the safe?"

Lord Claythorpe hesitated.

"Not that I know," he said. "Why, yes, of course, he had! I did not realize it. Yes, Remington had a key."

"And is this the key?" Peter Dawes handed his lordship a long steel key which he had taken from his pocket, and Lord Claythorpe examined it intently.

"Yes," he said, "that is undoubtedly one of the keys of the safe. Where did you find it?"

"Under the table," said the detective.

"Are there any other clues?" asked his lordship after a pause, and this time Peter did not immediately answer.

"Yes, there is one," he said. "We found in the dead man's hand a small visiting-card."

"What was the name?" asked the other quickly.

"The name was Mr. Jamieson Steele, who, I believe, was a former employee of yours."

"Steele! By heaven! That fits in with what I have been saying all along!" cried Claythorpe. "So Steele was in it!"

"It doesn't follow because this card was found in Remington's hand that the card belonged to the burglar," said Peter quietly. "It is not customary in criminal circles for murderers to leave their cards upon their victims, as I daresay your lordship knows."

Claythorpe looked at him sharply.

"This does not seem to me to be a moment when you can exercise your sarcasm at my expense," he growled. "I tell you Steele is a blackguard, and is the kind of man who would assist this notorious woman in her undertakings. Of course, if you're going to shield him——"

"I shield nobody," said Peter coldly. "I would not even shield your lordship if I had the slightest evidence against you. Of that you may be sure."

Lord Claythorpe winced.

"This is a heavy loss for you," said Peter, who was ignorant of the contents of the safe. Then, noticing the other's silence, he asked quickly: "You will, of course, give me the fullest information as to what the safe contained. And you can't do better than tell me now. Was it ready money?"

Lord Claythorpe shook his head.

"Nothing but securities," he said, "and those not of a negotiable character."

"Your securities?" asked Peter. "What was their value?"

"About a quarter of a million," said his lordship, and Peter gasped.

"Your money?" he asked again.

"No," hesitated Lord Claythorpe. "Not my money, but a trust fund——"

Peter sprang up from the table.

"You don't mean to say that this was the fortune of Miss Joyce Wilberforce about which we were talking this morning?"

His lordship nodded.

"It is," he said briefly. "It is a great tragedy, and I don't know how I shall excuse myself to the poor girl."

"You, of course, know what the securities were?" said Peter in a dry, matter-of-fact voice, as he sat down once more at the table.

In that moment he betrayed no more emotion than if he had been investigating the most commonplace of shop robberies.

"I have a list," said Claythorpe, and for nearly an hour he was detailing particulars of the bonds which had been stolen.

Peter finished his inquiry at four in the morning, and went to his office to send out an all-Britain message.

It was not like Jane, this latest crime. It was certainly not like Jane or her assistant—if she had an assistant—to leave an incriminating visiting-card in poor Remington's hand.

Peter Dawes was wise in the ways of criminals, both habitual and involuntary. He had seen a great deal of the grim side of his profession, and had made a careful study of anatomy, particularly in relation to murdered people. He was satisfied in his own mind that the card that was held in the lightly clenched fist of the dead man had been placed there after he had been shot.

He expressed himself frankly to his chief.

"The card is evidently a plant to lead us off the track; and if it was put there by Four Square Jane it was designed with the object of switching suspicion from her on to the unfortunate Steele."

"Do you think you'll catch Steele?" asked the chief.

55

Peter nodded.

"Yes, sir, I can catch him just when I want him, I think," he said. "It was only because we didn't want to take this man that we have let him go loose so long. He was a fool to run away, because the evidence against him was pretty paltry."

Dawes had a large number of calls to make the following morning, and the first of these was on a firm of safemakers in Queen Victoria Avenue. He had the good fortune to find that the sales manager had been in control of the store for the past twenty years, and that he remembered distinctly selling the safe to Lord Claythorpe.

"That's a relief," smiled the detective. "I was afraid I should have to go all over London to find the seller. How many keys did you supply?"

"Two," said the man. "One for his lordship, and one for Mr. Remington."

"Was there any difference in the two keys?"

"None except the marking. Have you one of the keys here?"

The detective produced it from his pocket, but when the salesman put out his hand for it he shook his head, with a smile.

"No, I'll keep it in my own hand, if you don't mind. I have a special reason," he said. "Perhaps you will describe the marking."

"It's inside the loop of the handle," explained the salesman. "You will find a small number engraved there—No. 1 or No. 2. No. 1 was intended for his lordship, No. 2 for Mr. Remington. The numbers were put there at Lord Claythorpe's suggestion in order to avoid confusion. It sometimes happens that both keys are in use together, and it is obviously desirable that they should not be mixed."

Peter looked at the inside of the loop and saw the number, then placed the key in his pocket with a little smile.

"Thank you; I think you have told me all that I want to know," he said. "You are sure that there are not three keys?"

"Perfectly certain," said the man emphatically. "And what is more, it would have been impossible to have got these keys cut, except by our firm."

Peter went back to Scotland Yard to find a telegram waiting for him. It was handed in at Falmouth by the chief of the local constabulary, and read:
—

"Jamieson Steele is here. Shall I arrest? We have undoubted evidence that he spent last night in Falmouth with his wife."

"His wife?" said the puzzled detective. "I didn't know Steele was married. Well, that lets him out as far as the murder's concerned. The question is shall we pinch him for the forgery?"

He consulted his friend the Inspector, and the advice he received with regard to the arrest on the lesser charge was emphatic.

"Leave him alone," said the wise man. "It does us no good to arrest a man unless we are certain of conviction, and the only real offence that Jamieson Steele has committed was the fool offence of running away when he ought to have stood his ground. I interviewed the bank manager immediately after that crime, and the bank manager swore that the signature was not a forgery, but was Lord Claythorpe's own; and with that evidence before the jury you're not going to get a conviction, young fellow!"

Peter debated this point, and at last decided to wire to Steele asking him to come up and meet him.

The papers were filled with the stories of Four Square Jane's latest exploit. This, indeed, was the culmination of a succession of sensational crimes. Her character, her eccentricities, the record of her several offences, appeared in every newspaper. There were witnesses who had seen a mysterious woman hurrying up St. James' Street a quarter of an hour after the crime must have been committed; there were others who were certain they saw a veiled woman getting into a car at the bottom of St. James' Street; in fact, the usual crop of rumours and evidence was forthcoming, none of which was of the slightest value to the police.

That afternoon the detective visited Lord Claythorpe. He found that gentleman in very close consultation with a grave Mr. Lewinstein. To the credit of that genial Hebrew financier it must be said that, however optimistic might be the prospectuses he framed from time to time, he was undoubtedly straight. And Mr. Lewinstein's gravity of demeanour was due to a doubt which had arisen in his mind for the first time as to the trustworthy character of his lordly business associate. They greeted the detective—his lordship suspiciously and a little nervously, Lewinstein with evident relief.

"Well," asked Claythorpe, "have you made any discovery?"

"Several," said Peter. "We have been able to reconstruct the crime up to a point, and we have also proved that Mr. Steele was in Falmouth when the murder was committed."

A little shade passed over the sallow face of Lord Claythorpe.

"How could you prove that when you don't know where he is?" he asked.

"We found where he was, all right," said Peter with satisfaction.

"And you have arrested him, of course?" demanded his lordship. "I mean for the forgery."

The other smiled.

"Honestly, Lord Claythorpe, do you seriously wish us to arrest Jamieson Steele, in view of the overwhelming evidence in support of his contention that the cheque was given to him by you, and signed by you?"

"It's a lie!" roared Lord Claythorpe, bringing his fist down on the table.

"It may be a lie," said Peter Dawes quietly, "but it is a lie the jury will believe, and I can't believe that the outcome of such a prosecution will be very profitable to your lordship."

Claythorpe was silent. Presently he looked up and caught Lewinstein's eye, and Lewinstein nodded.

"I quite agree," said that gentleman seriously. "I never thought there was much of a case against young Steele. He was a good boy. Why he got rattled and ran away heaven only knows."

Claythorpe changed the subject, which was wholly disagreeable to him.

"Have you found anything else?"

"Nothing except this," said Peter, taking a key from his pocket and laying it on the table before Lord Claythorpe. "Will you be kind enough to show me your key?"

Claythorpe looked at the other for fully a minute.

"Certainly," he said. He disappeared from the room and returned with a bunch of keys, on the end of which lay the facsimile of that which lay on the table.

Peter took the key and examined it. He looked at the inside of the loop, and as he did so an involuntary cry broke from Claythorpe's lips.

"A jumping tooth," he mumbled in apology. "Well, what have you found?"

"I've found that your keys have got slightly mixed," said Peter. "You have Remington's, and the key found in the office after the murder is yours!"

"Impossible!" said Lord Claythorpe.

"It is one of the impossible things that has happened," said Peter.

"Well, there's an explanation for that," Claythorpe began, but Peter stopped him.

"Of course there is," he said. "There are a hundred explanations, all of which are quite satisfactory. I suppose you had the keys out together on the table, and they got mixed at some time or other, and you did not notice. I'm not suggesting that you can't explain. I merely point out this fact, which at present has no bearing, or very little, or any aspect of the case."

Lewinstein and the detective went from the house together. His lordship, left alone, paced the study restlessly. Then he sat down at his desk and began to write. He produced two large canvas envelopes from the drawer of his desk, and into one of these he inserted a square certificate. He examined it casually before he put it into the cover. It was a debenture certificate issued by the North American Smelter Corporation for five hundred thousand dollars, and there was a particular reason why he should not have this valuable and important document in his house. He addressed the envelope containing the cover to himself in London. This he crossed with blue pencil, and from a drawer took out a small box containing a number of unused stamps. They were not British stamps, but Colonial, including Australian, African, Indian, and British Chinese. He fixed two Australian stamps, and placed the envelope within another, a little bigger. This he addressed to the manager of a Tasmanian bank, with whom he had done some business. To this gentleman he wrote a letter, saying that he expected to be in Australia by the time this letter reached it's destination.

"But," the letter went on, "if by any chance I am not able to get to Australia, and I do not call for this packet within a week after its arrival, or notify you by cable, asking you to keep it for me, will you please send it back to me by registered post."

That was a job well done, he thought, as he sealed the envelope. This incriminating document would at any rate be out of the country for three months. Should he register it? He scratched his chin dubiously. Registration literally meant registration. If people inquired as to whether he had made any important transfer by mail, there would be no difficulty in discovering, not only the fact that he had posted such a letter, but the address to which it had been posted. No, on the whole he thought it would be better if he sent the letter by ordinary post. He put on his hat and coat, and took the letter himself to the nearest post office. On his return his butler announced a visitor.

"Miss Wilberforce!" said his lordship in surprise, "I thought she was in the country."

"She arrived a few minutes after you left, m'lord."

"Excellent!" said Claythorpe. It was the last person he had expected to see, and he fetched a sigh of relief. It might have been awkward if she had arrived earlier—at any rate, it was a remarkable coincidence that she had come at all that evening.

He found her standing by his table, and went towards her with outstretched hands.

"My dear Joyce," he said, "whatever brings you here?"

"I had a telegram about the robbery," she said; and then for the first time he realized that he had not troubled to notify the only person who was really affected by the burglary.

"Who wired you?"

"The police."

Still he was puzzled.

"But you couldn't have had the wire till eleven," he said, "how on earth did you get here?"

She smiled rather quietly.

"I did rather an adventurous thing," she replied. "There is an aeroplane service between Falmouth and London."

He could only stare at her.

"That was very enterprising of you, Joyce."

"Tell me," she said, "did you also wire about this robbery?"

"I've been waiting till I got the fullest details before I notified you," said Lord Claythorpe easily. "You see, my dear girl, I have no wish to worry or frighten you, and possibly there was some chance that this wretched woman would return the securities, or at any rate give me a chance of redeeming them."

She nodded.

"I see," she said. "Then I can do nothing?"

He shook his head.

"Absolutely nothing."

She pursed her lips irresolutely.

"Can I write a letter?" she asked.

"Sit down, sit down, my dear child," he fussed. "You'll find paper and envelopes in this case."

* * * *

At eleven o'clock that night, South Western District Post Office No. 2 was a scene of animation. Postal vans, horse vans and motors were pulled up level with the big platform which led from the sorting room, and a dozen porters were engaged in handling mail bags for various destinations. The vans conveying local London mails had been despatched to the various district offices, the last to leave being a small one-horse van carrying the foreign mails to the G.P.O. It was driven by a middle-aged attendant named Carter, and pulled out of the yard at a quarter to twelve.

The weather was a repetition of that which had been experienced on the previous night. The south-wester was still blowing, the rain was coming down in gusty squalls, and the driver, muffled up to the chin, whipped up his horse to face the blast. His way led through the most deserted part of London's West End—more deserted than usual on this stormy night. One of the main streets through which he had to pass was "up," being in the hands of the road repairers, and he turned into a side street to make a detour which would bring him clear of the obstruction. He observed, as he again turned his horse into the narrow thoroughfare running parallel with the main road, that the street lamps were extinguished, and put this down to the storm. He was in the blackest patch of the road, when a red lamp flashed right ahead of him, and he pulled his horse back on its haunches.

"What's the trouble?" he said leaning down and addressing the figure that held the lamp.

For answer, a blinding ray of light, directed by a powerful pocket lamp, struck him full in the face, and before he realised what had happened, someone had leapt on to the wheel and was by his side, clutching at the rails on top of the van. Something cold and hard was pressed against his neck.

"Utter a sound and you're a dead man," said a man's voice.

A quarter of an hour later, all that stood for authority in London was searching for a dark low motor car, and Peter Dawes, sitting on the edge of his bed in his pyjamas, was eagerly questioning one of his junior officers over the 'phone.

"Robbed the mail? Impossible! How did it happen? Were they arrested? I'll be with you in ten minutes."

He slipped into a suit, buttoned his mackintosh, and stepped out into the wild night. His flat was opposite a cab rank, and in less than ten minutes he was at Scotland Yard.

"… the man said the thing was over so quickly he hadn't a chance of shouting, besides which, the fellow who stood by his side threatened to shoot him."

"What have they taken?"

"Only one bag, so far as can be ascertained. They knew just what they were after, and when they had got it they disappeared. The constable at the other end of the street heard the man shout, and came running down just in time to see a motor car turn the corner."

Later, Peter interviewed the driver, a badly scared man, in the stable-yard of the contractor who supplied the horses for the post office vans. The driver was a man who had been in the Government service for ten years, and had covered the route he was following that night—except that he had never previously taken the side street rendered necessary by the condition of the road—for the greater part of that time.

"Did you see anybody else except the man who sat by your side and threatened you?" asked Peter.

"Yes, sir," replied the man. "I saw what I thought was a girl in a black oilskin; she passed round to the back of the van."

"Where is the van? Is it here?" asked the detective, and they showed him a small, four-wheeled vehicle, covered in at the top and with two doors which were fastened behind by a steel bar and padlocked. The padlock had been wrenched open, and the doors now stood ajar.

"They had taken out the mail bags, sir, in order to sort them out to see what was gone."

Peter flashed his lamp in the interior, examining the floor and sides carefully. There was no clue of any kind until he began his inspection of the inside of the doors, and there, on the very centre, was the familiar label.

"Four Square Jane, eh?" said Peter, and whistled.

CHAPTER 7

"I deeply regret that I found it necessary to interfere with His Majesty's mails. In a certain bag was a letter which was very compromising to me, and it was necessary that I should recover it. I beg to enclose the remainder of the letters which are, as you will see, intact and untampered with!"

This document, bearing the seal manual of Four Square Jane, was delivered to the Central Post Office accompanied by a large mail bag. The person who delivered it was a small boy of the District Messenger Service, who brought the package in a taxi-cab. He could give no information as to the person who had sent him except to say that it was a lady wearing a heavy veil, who had summoned him to a popular hotel, and had met him in the vestibule. They had taken a cab together, and at the corner of Clarges Street the cab had pulled up on the instructions of the lady; a man had appeared bearing a bundle that he had put into a cab which then drove on. A little later the lady had stopped the cab, given the boy a pound note, and herself descended. The boy could only say that in his opinion she was young, and undoubtedly in mourning.

Here was new fuel to the flames of excitement which the murder of Remington had aroused. A murder one day, accompanied by a robbery which, if rumour had any foundation, involved nearly a quarter of a million pounds, and this tragedy followed on the next day by the robbery of the King's mail; and all at the hands of a mysterious woman whose name was already a household word—these happenings apart from the earlier crimes were sufficient to furnish not only London but the whole of Britain with a subject for discussion.

Lord Claythorpe heard the news of the robbery with some uneasiness. Inquiries made at the local district office however, relieved him of his anxiety. The mail bag which had been taken, he was informed, was part of the Indian mail. The Australian mail had been delivered at the General Post Office earlier in the evening by the service which left the district office at nine o'clock. It was as well for his peace of mind that he did not know how erroneous was the information he had been given. He had asked Joyce to breakfast with him, and had kept her waiting whilst he pursued these inquiries; for he had read of the robbery in bed, and had hurried round to the district office without delay.

"This is the most amazing exploit of all," he said to the girl, as he handed her the paper. "Take this," he said. "I have read it."

"Poor Jane Briglow!"

"Why Jane Briglow?"

The girl smiled.

"Mother insists that it is she who has committed all these acts. As a matter of fact, I happen to know that Jane is in good service in the North of England."

Claythorpe looked at her in surprise.

"Is that so?" he said incredulously. "Do you know, I'd begun to form a theory about that girl."

"Well, don't," said Joyce, helping herself to jam.

"I wonder whether they'll get the bag back," speculated his lordship. "There's nothing about it in the papers."

"It is very unlikely, I should think," said Joyce. She rolled up her table-napkin. "You wanted to see me about something this morning," she said.

He nodded.

"Yes, Joyce," he said. "I've been thinking matters over. I'm afraid I was rather prejudiced against young Steele." The girl made no reply. "I'm not even certain that he was guilty of the offence with which I charged him," Claythorpe went on. "You see, I was very worried at the time, and it is possible that I may have signed a cheque and overlooked the fact. You were very fond of Steele?"

She nodded.

"Well," said Lord Claythorpe heartily, "I will no longer stand in your way."

She looked at him steadily.

"You mean you will consent to my marriage?"

He nodded.

"Why not?" he asked.

"Why not, indeed?" she said, a little bitterly. "I understand that my fortune no longer depends upon whether I marry according to your wishes or not—since I have no fortune."

"It is very deplorable," said his lordship gravely. "Really, I feel morally responsible. It is a most stupendous tragedy, but I will do whatever I can to make it up to you, Joyce. I am not a rich man by any means, but I have decided, if you still feel you cannot marry my son, and would prefer to marry Mr. Steele, to give you a wedding gift of twenty thousand pounds."

"That is very good of you," said the girl politely, "but, of course, I cannot take your verbal permission. You will not mind putting that into writing?"

"With all the pleasure in life," said Lord Claythorpe, getting up and walking to a writing-table, "really Joyce, you're becoming quite shrewd in your old age," he chuckled.

He drew a sheet of paper from a writing-case and poised a pen.

"What is the date?" he asked.

"It is the nineteenth," said the girl. "But date it as from the first of the month."

"Why?" he asked in surprise.

"Well, there are many reasons," said the girl slowly. "I shouldn't like people to think, for example, that your liking for Mr. Steele dated from the loss of my property."

He looked at her sharply, but not a muscle of her face moved.

"That is very considerate of you," he said with a shrug, "and it doesn't really matter whether I make it the first or the twenty-first, does it?"

He wrote quickly, blotted the sheet, handed it to the girl, and she read it and folded the paper away in her handbag.

"Was that really the reason you asked me to date the permission back?" he asked curiously.

She shook her head.

"No," she said coolly. "I was married to Jamieson last week."

"Married!" he gasped. "Without my permission!"

"With your permission," she said, tapping her little bag.

For a second he frowned, and then he burst into a roar of laughter.

"Well, well," he said. "That's rather rich. You're a very naughty girl, Joyce. Does your mother know?"

"Mother knows nothing about it," said the girl. "There is one more thing I want to speak to you about, Lord Claythorpe, and that is in connection with the robbery of the mail last night."

It was at that moment that Peter Dawes was announced.

"It's the detective," said Lord Claythorpe with a little frown. "You don't want to see him?"

"On the contrary, let him come in, because what I am going to say will interest him," she said.

Claythorpe nodded to the butler, and a few seconds later Peter Dawes came into the room. He bowed to the girl and shook hands with Lord Claythorpe.

"This is my niece—well, not exactly my niece," smiled Claythorpe, "but the niece of a very dear friend of mine, and, in fact, the lady who is the principal loser in that terrible tragedy of St. James' Street."

"Indeed?" said Peter with a smile. "I think I know the young lady by sight."

"And she was going to make an interesting communication to me just as you came in," said Claythorpe. "Perhaps, Joyce, dear, you will tell Mr. Dawes?"

"I was only going to say that this morning I received this." She did not go to her bag, but produced a folded paper from the inside of her blouse. This she opened and spread on the table and Claythorpe's face went white, for it was the five hundred thousand dollar bond which he had despatched the day before to Australia. "I seem to remember," said the girl, "that this was part of my inheritance—you remember I was given a list of the securities you held for me?"

Lord Claythorpe licked his dry lips.

"Yes," he said huskily. "That is part of your inheritance."

"How did it come to you?" asked Peter Dawes.

"It was found in my letter-box this morning," said the girl.

"Accompanied by a letter?"

"No, nothing," said Joyce. "For some reason I connected it with the mail robbery, and thought that perhaps you had entrusted this certificate to the post—and that in your letter you mentioned the fact that it was mine."

"That also is impossible," said Peter Dawes quietly, "because, if your statement is correct, this document would have been amongst those which were stolen on the night that Remington was murdered. Isn't that so, Lord Claythorpe?"

Claythorpe nodded.

"It is very providential for you, Joyce," he said huskily. "I haven't the slightest idea how it came to you. Probably the thief who murdered Remington knew it was yours and restored it."

The girl nodded.

"The thief being Four Square Jane, eh?" said Peter Dawes, eyeing his lordship narrowly.

"Naturally, who else?" said Claythorpe, meeting the other's eyes steadily. "It was undoubtedly her work, her label was on the inside of the safe."

"That is true," agreed Peter. "But there was one remarkable fact about that label which seems to have been overlooked."

"What was that?"

"It had been used before," said Peter slowly. "It was an old label which had previously been attached to something or somewhere, for the marks of the old adhesion were still on it when I took it off. In fact, there were only a few places where the gum on the label remained useful."

Neither the eyes of the girl or Lord Claythorpe left the other's face.

"That is curious," said Lord Claythorpe slowly. "What do you deduce from that?"

Dawes shrugged.

"Nothing, except that it is possible someone is using Four Square Jane's name in vain," he said, "someone who was in a position to get one of the old labels she had used on her previous felonies. May I sit down?" he asked, for he had not been invited to take a seat.

Claythorpe nodded curtly, and Dawes pulled a chair from the table and seated himself.

"I have been reconstructing that crime," he said, "and there are one or two things that puzzle me. In the first place, I am perfectly certain that no woman was in your office on the night the murder was committed."

Lord Claythorpe raised his eyebrows.

"Indeed!" he said. "And yet the constable who was first in the room told me that he distinctly smelt a very powerful scent—the sort a woman would use. I also noticed it when I went into the room."

"So did I," said Peter, "and that quite decided me that Four Square Jane had nothing to do with the business. A cool, calculating woman like Four Square Jane is certain to be a lady of more than ordinary intelligence and regular habits. She is not the kind who would suddenly take up a powerful scent, because it is possible to trace a woman criminal by this means, and it is certain that in no other case which is associated with her name was there the slightest trace or hint of perfume. That makes me more certain that the crime was committed by a man and that he sprinkled the scent on the floor in order to leave the impression that Four Square Jane had been the operator."

"What do you think happened?" asked Lord Claythorpe after a pause.

"I think that Remington went to the office with the intention of examining the contents of the safe," said Peter deliberately. "I believe he had the whole of the envelopes on the table, and had opened several, when he was surprised by somebody who came into the office. There was an argument, in the course of which he was shot dead."

"You suggest that the intruder was a burglar?" said Lord Claythorpe with a set face, but Peter shook his head.

"No," he said. "This man admitted himself to the office by means of a key. The door was not forced, and there was no sign of a skeleton key having been used. Moreover, the newcomer must have been well acquainted with the office, because, after the murder was committed he switched out the light and pulled up the blinds which Remington had lowered, so that the light should not attract attention from the street. We know they were lowered, because the constable on beat duty on the other side of the street saw no sign of a light. The blinds were heavy and practically light-proof. Now, the man who committed the murder knew his way about the office well enough to turn out the light, move in the dark, and manipulate the three blinds which covered the windows. I've been experimenting with those blinds, and I've found that they're fairly complicated in their mechanism."

Again there was a pause.

"A very fantastic theory, if you will allow me to say so," said Lord Claythorpe, "and not at all like the sensible, commonsense point of view that I should have expected from Scotland Yard."

"That may be so," said Peter quietly. "But we get romantic theories even at Scotland Yard."

He looked down at the bond, still spread out on the table.

"I suppose your lordship will put this in the bank after your unhappy experience?" he said.

"Yes, yes," said Lord Claythorpe briefly, and Peter turned to the girl.

"I congratulate you upon recovering a part of your property," he said. "I understand this is held in trust for you until you're married."

Lord Claythorpe started violently.

"Until you're married!" he said. "Why, why!" He caught the girl's smiling eyes. "That means now, doesn't it?" he said.

"Until your marriage is approved by me," said Lord Claythorpe.

"I think it is approved by you," said Joyce, and dived her hand into her bag.

"It will be delivered to you formally tomorrow," said his lordship stiffly.

Peter Dawes and the girl went out of the house together and walked in silence a little way.

"I'd give a lot to know what you're thinking," said the girl.

"And I'd give a lot to know what you know," smiled Peter, and at that cryptic exchange they parted.

That night Mr. Lewinstein was giving a big dinner party at the Ritz Carlton. Joyce had been invited months before, but had no thought of accepting the invitation until she returned to the hotel where she was staying.

A good-looking man rose as she entered the vestibule, and came towards her with a smile. He took her arm, and slowly they paced the long corridor leading to the elevator.

"So that's Mr. Jamieson Steele, eh?" said Peter Dawes, who had followed her to the hotel, and he looked very thoughtfully in the direction the two had taken.

He went from the hotel and called on Mr. Lewinstein by appointment, and that great financier welcomed him with a large cigar.

"I heard you were engaged upon the Four Square Jane case, Mr. Dawes," he said, "and I thought it wouldn't be a bad idea if I invited you to dinner tonight."

"Is this a professional or a friendly engagement?" smiled Peter.

"It's both," said Mr. Lewinstein frankly. "The fact is, Mr. Dawes, and I'm not going to make any bones about the truth, it is necessary in my business that I should keep in touch with the best people in London. From time to time I give a dinner-party, and I bring together all that is bright and beautiful and brainy. Usually these dinners are given in my own house, but I've had a rather painful experience," he said grimly, and Peter, who knew the history of Four Square Jane's robbery, nodded in sympathy.

"Now, I want to say a few words about Miss Four Square Jane," said Lewinstein. "Do you mind seeing if the door is closed?"

Peter looked outside, and closed the door carefully.

"I'd hate what I'm saying to be repeated in certain quarters," Lewinstein went on. "But in that robbery there were several remarkable coincidences. Do you know that Four Square Jane stole nothing, in most cases, except the presents that had been given by Claythorpe? Claythorpe is rather a gay old bird and has gone the pace. He has been spending money like water for years. Of course, he may have a big income, or he may not. I know just what he gets out of the City. On the night of the burglary at my house this girl went through every room and took articles which in many cases had been given to the various people by Claythorpe. For example, something he had presented to my wife disappeared; some shirt-studs, which he gave to me, were also gone. That's rather funny, don't you think?"

"It fits in with my theory," said Peter nodding, "that Four Square Jane has only one enemy in the world, and that is Lord Claythorpe."

"That's my opinion, too," said Lewinstein. "Now tonight I am giving a big dinner-party, as I told you, and there will be a lot of women there, and the women are scared of my parties since the last one. There will be jewels to burn, but what makes me specially nervous is that Claythorpe has insisted on Lola Lane being invited."

"The dancer?" asked Peter in surprise, and the other nodded.

"She's a great friend of Claythorpe's—I suppose you know that? He put up the money for her last production, and, not to put too fine a point upon it, the old man is infatuated by the girl."

Mr. Lewinstein sucked contemplatively at one of his large cigars.

"I am not a prude, you understand, Mr. Dawes," he said, "and the way men amuse themselves does not concern me. Claythorpe is much too big a man for me to refuse any request he makes. In the present state of society, people like Lola are accepted, and it is not for me to reform the Smart Set. The only thing I'm scared about is that she will be covered from head to foot in jewels."

He pulled again at his cigar, and looked at it before he went on:

"Which Lord Claythorpe has given her."

"This is news to me," said Peter.

"It would be news to a lot of people," said Lewinstein, "for Claythorpe is supposed to be one of the big moral forces in the City." He chuckled, as though at a good joke. "Now, there's another point I want to make to you. This girl Lola has been telling her friends—at least, she told a friend of mine—that she was going to the Argentine to live in about six months' time. My friend asked her if Lord Claythorpe agreed to that arrangement. You know, these theatrical people are very frank, and she said 'Yes.'" He looked at the detective.

"Which means that Claythorpe is going, too," said Peter, and Lewinstein nodded.

"That is also news," said Peter Dawes. "Thank you, I will accept your invitation to dinner tonight."

"Good!" said Lewinstein, brightening. "You don't mind, but I may have to put you next to Lola."

That evening when Peter strolled into the big reception hall which Mr. Lewinstein had engaged with his private dining-room, his eyes wandered in search of the lady. He knew her by sight—had seen her picture in the illustrated newspapers. He had no difficulty in distinguishing her rather bold features; and, even if he had not, he would have known, from the daring dress she wore, that this was the redoubtable lady whose name had been hinted in connection with one or two unpleasant scandals.

But chiefly his eyes were for the great collar of emeralds about her shapely throat. They were big green stones which scintillated in the shaded lights, and were by far the most remarkable jewels in the room. Evidently Lewinstein had explained to Lord Claythorpe the reason of the invitation, because his lordship received him quite graciously and made no demur at a common detective occupying the place by the side of the lady who had so completely enthralled him.

It was after the introduction that Peter had a surprise, for he saw Joyce Wilberforce.

"I didn't expect to see you again today, Miss Wilberforce," he said.

"I did not expect to come myself," replied the girl, "but my husband—you knew I was married?"

Mr. Dawes nodded.

"That is one of the things I did know," he laughed.

"My husband had an engagement, and he suggested that I should amuse myself by coming here. What do you think of the emeralds?" she asked mischievously. "I suppose you're here to keep a friendly eye on them?"

Peter smiled.

"They are rather gorgeous, aren't they? Though I cannot say I admire their wearer."

Peter was discreetly silent. He took the dancer in to dinner, and found her a singularly dull person, except on the question of dress and the weakness of her sister artistes. The dinner was in full swing when Joyce Wilberforce, who was sitting almost opposite the detective, screamed and hunched herself up in the chair.

"Look, look!" she cried, pointing to the floor. "A rat!"

Peter, leaning over the table, saw a small brown shape run along the wainscot. The woman at his side shrieked and drew her feet up to the rail of her chair. This was the last thing he saw, for at that second all the lights in the room went out. He heard a scream from the dancer.

"My necklace, my necklace!"

There was a babble of voices, a discordant shouting of instructions and advice. Then Peter struck a match. The only thing he saw in the flickering light was the figure of Lola, with her hands clasped round her neck.

The collar of emeralds had disappeared!

It was five minutes before somebody fixed the fuse and brought the lights on again.

"Let nobody leave the room!" shouted Peter authoritatively. "Everybody here must be searched. And——"

Then his eyes fell upon a little card which had been placed on the table before him, and which had not been there when the lights went out. There was no need to turn it. He knew what to expect on the other side. The four squares and the little J looked up at him mockingly.

71

CHAPTER 8

Peter Dawes, of Scotland Yard, had to do some mighty quick thinking and, by an effort of will, concentrate his mind upon all the events which had immediately preceded the robbery of the dancer's necklace. First there was Joyce Wilberforce, who had undoubtedly seen a rat running along by the wainscot, and had drawn up her feet in a characteristically feminine fashion. Then he had seen the dancer draw up her feet, and put down her hands to pull her skirts tight—also a characteristically feminine action.

What else had he seen? He had seen a hand, the hand of a waiter, between himself and the woman on his left. He remembered now that there was something peculiar about that hand which had attracted his attention, and that he had been on the point of turning his head in order to see it better when Joyce's scream had distracted his attention.

What was there about that hand? He concentrated all his mind upon this trivial matter, realising instinctively that behind that momentary omen was a possible solution of the mystery. He remembered that it was a well-manicured hand. That in itself was remarkable in a waiter. There had been no jewels or rings upon it, which was not remarkable. This he had observed idly. Then, in a flash, the detail which had interested him came back to his mind. The little finger was remarkably short. He puzzled his head to connect this malformation with something he had heard before. Leaving the room in the charge of the police who had been summoned, he took a taxi and drove straight to the hotel where Joyce Steele was staying with her husband.

"Mrs. Steele is out, but Mr. Steele has just come in," said the hotel clerk. "Shall I send your name up?"

"It is unnecessary," said the detective, showing his card. "I will go up to his room. What is the number?"

He was told, and a page piloted him to the door. Without troubling to knock, he turned the handle and walked in. Jamieson Steele was sitting before a little fire, smoking a cigarette, and looked up at the intruder.

"Hullo, Mr. Dawes," he said calmly.

"You know me, eh?" said Peter. "May I have a few words with you?"

"You can have as many as you like," said Steele. "Take a chair, won't you? This is not a bad little sitting-room, but it is rather draughty. To what am I indebted for this visit? Is our wicked uncle pressing his charge of forgery?"

Peter Dawes smiled.

"I don't think that is likely," he said. "I have made a call upon you for the purpose of seeing your hands."

"My hands?" said the other in a tone of surprise. "Are you going in for a manicure?"

"Hardly," said Peter drily, as the other spread out his hands before him. "What is the matter with your little finger?" he asked, after a scrutiny.

Jamieson Steele examined the finger and laughed.

"He is not very big, is he?" he laughed. "Arrested development, I suppose. It is the one blemish on an otherwise perfect body."

"Where have you been tonight?" asked Peter quietly.

"I have been to various places, including Scotland Yard?" was the staggering reply.

"To Scotland Yard?" asked Peter incredulously, and Jamieson Steele nodded.

"The fact is, I wanted to see you about the curious charge which Lord Claythorpe brings forward from time to time; and also I felt that some explanation was due to you as you are in charge of a case which nearly affects my wife, as to the reason I did a bolt when Claythorpe brought this charge of forgery against me."

"What time did you leave the Yard?"

"About half an hour ago," said Steele.

Peter looked at him closely. He was wearing an ordinary lounge suit, and a soft shirt. The hand which had come upon the table had undoubtedly been encased in a stiff cuff and a black sleeve.

"Why, what is the matter?" asked Steele.

"There has been a robbery at the Ritz Carlton tonight," Peter explained. "A man dressed as a waiter has stolen an emerald necklace."

"And naturally you suspect me," he said ironically. "Well, you're at liberty to search this apartment."

"May I see your dress clothes?" said Peter.

For answer, the other led him to his bedroom, and his dress suit was discovered at the bottom of a trunk, carefully folded and brushed.

"Now," said Peter, "if you don't mind, I'll conduct the search you suggest. You understand that I have no authority to do so, and I can only make the search with your permission."

"You have my permission," said the other. "I realise that I am a suspected person, so go ahead, and don't mind hurting my feelings."

Peter's search was thorough, but revealed nothing of importance.

"This is my wife's room," said Steele. "Perhaps you would like to search that?"

"I should," said Peter Dawes, without hesitation, but again his investigations drew blank.

He opened all the windows of the room, feeling along the window-sills for a tape, cord or thread, from which an emerald necklace might be suspended. It was an old trick to fasten a stolen article to a black thread, and the black thread to some stout gummed paper fastened to the window-sill; but here again he discovered nothing.

"Now," said the cheerful young man, "you had better search me."

"I might as well do the job thoroughly," agreed Peter, and ran his hands scientifically over the other's body.

"Not guilty, eh?" said Steele, when he had finished. "Now perhaps you'll sit down, and I'll tell you something about Lord Claythorpe that will interest you. You know, of course, that Claythorpe has been living on the verge of bankruptcy. Won't you sit down?" he said again, and Peter obeyed. "Here is a cigar which will steady your nerves."

"I can't stay very long," said Peter, "but I should like your end of the serial very much indeed."

He took the proffered cigar, and bit off the end.

"As I was saying," Steele went on, "Claythorpe has been living for years on the verge of bankruptcy. He is a man who, from his youth up, has been dependent on his wits. His early life was passed in what the good books called dissolute living. I believe there was a time when he was so broke he slept on the Embankment."

Peter nodded. He also had heard something to this effect.

"This, of course, was before he came into the title. He is a clever and unscrupulous man with a good address. And knowing that he was up against it, he set himself to gain powerful friends. One of these friends was my wife's uncle—a good-natured innocent kind of man, who had amassed a considerable fortune in South Africa. I believe Claythorpe bled him pretty considerably, and might have bled him to death, only the old fellow died naturally, leaving a handsome legacy to his friends and the residue of his property to my wife. Claythorpe was made the executor, and given pretty wide powers. Amongst the property which my wife inherited—or rather, would inherit on her wedding day, was a small coal-mine in the North of England, which at the time of the old man's death was being managed by a very brilliant young engineer, whose name modesty alone prevents my revealing."

"Go on," said Peter, with a smile.

"Claythorpe, finding himself in control of such unlimited wealth, set himself out to improve the property. And the first thing he did was to project the flotation of my coal mine—I call it mine, and I always regarded it as such in a spiritual sense—for about six times its value."

Peter nodded.

"In order to bring in the public, it was necessary that a statement should be made with regard to the quantity of coal in the mine, the extent of the seams, etc., and it was my duty to prepare a most glowing statement, which would loosen the purse-strings of the investing public. Claythorpe put the scheme up to me, and I said, 'No.' I also told him," the young man went on, choosing his words carefully, "that, if he floated this company, I should have something to say in the columns of the financial Press. So the thing was dropped, but Claythorpe never forgave me. There was a certain work which I had done for him outside my ordinary duties and, summoning me to his St. James' Street office, he gave me a cheque. I noticed at the time that the cheque was for a much larger amount than I had expected, and thought his lordship was trying to get into my good books. I also noticed that the amount inscribed on the cheque had the appearance of being altered, and that even his lordship's signature looked rather unusual. I took the cheque and presented it to my bank a few days later, and was summoned to the office, where I was denounced as a forger," said the young man, puffing a ring of smoke into the air reflectively, "but it gives you a very funny feeling in the pit of the stomach. The heroic and proper and sensible thing to do was to stand on my ground, go up to the Old Bailey, make a great speech which would call forth the applause and approbation of judge and jury, and stalk out of the court in triumph. Under these circumstances, however, one seldom does the proper thing. Remington it was—the man who is now dead—who suggested that I should bolt; and, like a fool, I bolted. The only person who knew where I was was Joyce. I won't tell you anything about my wife, because you probably know everything that is worth knowing. I'll only say that I've loved her for years, and that my affection has been returned. It was she who urged me to come back to London and stand my trial, but I put this down to her child-like innocence—a man is always inclined to think that he's the cleverer of the two when he's exchanging advice with women. That's the whole of the story."

Peter waited.

"Now, Mr. Steele," he said, "perhaps you will explain why you were at the Ritz-Carlton Hotel tonight disguised as a waiter."

Steele looked at him with a quizzical smile.

"I think I could explain it if I'd been there," he said. "Do you want me to invent an explanation as well as to invent my presence?"

"I am as confident that you were there," said Peter, "as I am that you are sitting here. I am also certain that it will be next to impossible to prove that you were in the room." He rose from his seat. "I am going back to the hotel," he said, "though I do not expect that any of our bloodhounds have discovered the necklace."

"Have another cigar," said Steele, offering the open box.

Peter shook his head.

"No thank you," he said.

"They won't hurt you, take a handful."

Peter laughingly refused.

"I think I am nearly through with this Four Square Jane business," he said, "and I am pretty certain that it is not going to bring kudos or promotion to me."

"I have a feeling that it will not, either," said Steele. "It's a rum case."

Peter shook his head.

"Rum, because I've solved the mystery of Four Square Jane. I know who she is, and why she has robbed Claythorpe and his friends."

"You know her, do you?" said Steele thoughtfully, and the other nodded.

Jamieson Steele waited till the door closed upon the detective, and then waited another five minutes before he rose and shot the bolt. He then locked the two doors leading from the sitting-room, took up the box of cigars and placed it on the table. He dipped into the box, and pulled out handful after handful of cigars, and then he took out something which glittered and scintillated in the light—a great collar of big emeralds—and laid it on the table. He looked at it thoughtfully, then wrapped it in a silk handkerchief and thrust it into his pocket, replacing the cigars in the box. He passed into his bedroom, and came out wearing a soft felt hat, and a long dark-blue trench coat.

He hesitated before he unbolted the door, unbuttoned the coat, and took out the handkerchief containing the emerald collar, and put it into his overcoat pocket. If he had turned his head at that moment, and looked at the half-opened door of his bedroom, he might have caught a glimpse of a figure that was watching his every movement. Peter Dawes had not come alone, and there were three entrances to the private suite which Mr. and Mrs. Steele occupied.

Then Jamieson Steele stepped out so quickly that by the time the watcher was in the corridor, he had disappeared down the lift, which happened to be going down at that moment. The man raced down the stairs three at a time. The last landing was a broad marble balcony which overlooked the hall, and, glancing down, he saw Peter waiting. He waved his hand significantly, and at that moment the elevator reached the ground floor, and Jamieson Steele stepped out of it.

He was half way across the vestibule when Peter confronted him.

"Wait a moment, Mr. Steele. I want you," said Peter.

It was at that second that the swing doors turned and Joyce Steele came in.

"Want me?" said Steele. "Why?"

"I am going to take you into custody on the charge of being concerned in the robbery tonight," said the detective.

"You're mad," said Steele, with an immovable face.

"Arrest him? Oh no, no!" It was the gasping voice of the girl. In a second she had flung herself upon the man, her two arms about him. "It isn't true, it isn't true!" she sobbed.

Very gently Steele pushed her back.

"Go away, my dear. This is no place for you," he said. "Mr. Dawes has made a great mistake, as he will discover."

The watcher had joined the group now.

"He's got the goods, sir," he said triumphantly. "I watched him. The necklace was in a cigar box. He has got it in his pocket."

"Hold out your hands," said Peter, and in a second Jamieson Steele was handcuffed.

"May I come?" said the girl.

"It is better you did not," said Peter. "Perhaps your husband will be able to prove his innocence. Anyway, you can do nothing."

They left her, a disconsolate figure, standing in the hall, and carried their prisoner to Cannon Row.

"Now we'll search you, if you don't mind?" asked Peter.

"Not at all," said the other coolly.

"Where did you say he put it?"

"In his pocket, sir," said the spy.

Peter searched the overcoat pockets.

"There's nothing here," he said.

"Nothing there?" gasped the man in astonishment. "But I saw him put it there. He took it out of his hip pocket and——"

"Well, let's try his hip pocket. Take off your coat, Steele."

The young man obeyed, and again Peter's deft fingers went over him, but with no better result. The two detectives looked at one another in consternation.

"A slight mistake on your part, my friend," said Peter, "I'm sorry we've given you all this trouble."

"Look in the bottom of the cab," the second detective pleaded, and Peter laughed.

"I don't see what he could do. He had the bracelets on his hands, and I never took my eyes off them once. You can search the cab if you like—it's waiting at the door."

But the search of the cab produced no better result.

And then an inspiration dawned upon Peter, and he laughed, softly and long.

"I'm going to give up this business," he said. "I really am, Steele. I'm too childishly trustful."

Their eyes met, and both eyes were creased with laughter.

"All right," said Peter. "Let him go."

"Let him go?" said the other detective in dismay.

"Yes. We've no evidence against this gentleman, and we're very unlikely to secure it."

For in that short space of time, Peter had realized exactly the kind he was up against; saw as clearly as daylight what had happened to the emeralds, and knew that any attempt to find them now would merely lead to another disappointment.

"If you don't mind, Steele, I think I'll go back with you to your hotel. I hope you're not bearing malice."

"Not at all," replied Steele. "It's your job to catch me, and my job to ——" he paused.

"Yes?" said Peter curiously.

"My job to get caught, obviously," said Steele with a laugh.

They did not speak again until they were in the cab on the way back to the hotel.

"I'm afraid my poor wife is very much upset."

"I'm not worrying about that," said Peter drily. "Steele, I think you are a wise man; and, being wise, you will not be averse to receiving advice from one who knows this game from A to Z."

Steele did not reply.

"My advice to you is, get out of the country just as soon as you can, and take your wife with you," said Peter. "There is an old adage that the pitcher goes often to the well—I need not remind you of that."

"Suppose I tell you I do not understand you," said Steele.

"You, will do nothing so banal," replied Peter. "I tell you I know your game, and the thing that is going to stand against you is the robbery of the mail. That is your only bad offence in my eyes, and it is the one for which I would work night and day to bring you to justice."

Again a silence.

"Nothing was stolen from the mail, that I know," said Peter. "It was all returned. Your principal offence is that you scared a respectable servant of his Majesty into fits. Anyway, it is a felony of a most serious kind, and would get you twenty years if we could secure evidence against you. You held up his Majesty's mail with a loaded revolver——"

"Even that you couldn't prove," laughed Steele. "It might not have been any more than a piece of gaspipe. After all, a hardened criminal, such as you believe I am, possessed of a brain which you must know by this time I have, would have sufficient knowledge of the law to prevent his carrying lethal weapons."

"We are talking here without witnesses," said Peter.

"I'm not so sure," said Steele quickly. "I thought I was talking to you in my little sitting-room without witnesses."

"Anyway, you can be sure there are no witnesses here," smiled Peter, as the cab turned into the street where the hotel was situated. "And I am asking you confidentially, and man to man, if you can give me any information at all regarding the murder in St. James' Street."

Steele thought awhile.

"I can't," he said. "As a matter of fact, I was in Falmouth at the time, as you know. Obviously, it was not the work of the lady who calls herself Four Square Jane, because my impression of that charming creature is that she would be scared to death at the sight of a revolver. The card which was found in the dead man's hand——"

"How did you know that?" asked Peter quickly.

"These things get about," replied the other unabashed. "Has it occurred to you that it was a moist night, that the murderer may have been hot, and that on the card may be his fingerprints?"

"That did occur to me," said Peter. "In fact, it was the first thing I thought about. And, if it is any interest to you, I will tell you that there was a finger print upon that card, which I have been trying for the past few days to——" He stopped. "Here we are at your hotel," he said. "There's a good detective lost in you, Steele."

"Not lost, but gone before," said the other flippantly. "Good-night. You won't come up and have a cigar?"

"No thanks," said a grim Peter.

He went back to Scotland Yard. It was curious, amazingly curious, that Steele should have mentioned the card that night. It was not into an empty office that he went, despite the lateness of the hour. There was an important police conference, and all the heads of departments were crowded into the room, the air of which was blue with tobacco smoke. A stout, genial man nodded to Peter as he came in.

"We've had a devil of a job getting it, Peter, but we've succeeded."

Before him was a small visiting-card, bearing the name of Jamieson Steele. In the very centre was a violet finger print. The finger print had not been visible to the naked eye until it had been treated with chemicals, and its present appearance was the result of the patient work of three of Scotland Yard's greatest scientists.

"Did you get the other?" said Peter.

"There it is," said the stout man, and pointed to a strip of cardboard bearing two black finger prints.

Peter compared the two impressions.

"Well," he said, "at any rate, one of the mysteries is cleared up. How did you get this?" he asked pointing to the strip of cardboard bearing the two prints.

"I called on him, and shook hands with him," said the stout man with a smile. "He was horribly surprised and offended that I should take such a liberty. Then I handed him the strip of card. It was a little while later, when he put his hand on the blotting pad, that he discovered that his palm and fingertips were black, and I think that he was the most astonished man I ever saw."

Peter smiled.

"He didn't guess that your hand would be carefully covered with lamp-black, I gather?"

"Hardly," said the fat man.

Again Peter compared the two impressions.

"There is no doubt at all about it," he said. He looked at his watch. "Half-past twelve. Not a bad time, either. I'll take Wilkins and Browne," he said, "and get the thing over. It's going to be a lot of trouble. Have you got the warrant?"

The stout man opened the drawer of his desk and passed a sheet of paper across. Peter examined it.

"Thank you," he said simply.

Lord Claythorpe was in his study taking a stiff whisky and soda when the detective was announced.

"Well?" he said. "Have you found the person who stole the emerald necklace?"

"No, my lord," said Peter. "But I have found the man who shot Remington."

Lord Claythorpe's face went ashen.

"What do you mean?" he said hoarsely "What do you mean?"

"I mean," said Peter, "that I am going to take you into custody on a charge of wilful murder, and I caution you that what you now say will be used in evidence against you."

CHAPTER 9

At three o'clock in the morning, Lord Claythorpe, an inmate of a cell at Cannon Row, sent for Peter Dawes. Peter was ushered into the cell, and found that Claythorpe had recovered from the crushed and hopeless man he had left: he was now calm and normal.

"I want to see you, Dawes," he said, "to clear up a few matters which are on my conscience."

"Of course, you know," said Peter, "that any statement you make——"

"I know, I know," said the other impatiently. "But I have this to say." He paced the short cell, his hands gripped behind him. Presently he sat down at Peter's side. "In the first place," he said, "let me tell you that I killed Donald Remington. There's a long story leading up to that killing, but I swear I had no intention of hurting him."

Peter had taken a notebook from one pocket and a pencil from another, and was jotting down in his queer shorthand the story the other told. Usually such a proceeding had the effect of silencing the man whose words were being inscribed, but Claythorpe did not seem to notice.

"When Joyce Wilberforce's uncle left me executor of his estate, I had every intention of going straight," he went on. "But I made bad losses in the Kaffir market, and gradually I began to nibble at her fortune. The securities, which were kept in sealed envelopes at the bank, were taken out one by one, and disposed of; blank sheets of paper were placed in the envelopes, which were resealed. And when the burglary occurred, there was only one hundred-thousand pound bond left. That bond you will find in a secret drawer of my desk. I think Remington, who was in my confidence except for this matter, suspected it all along. When I took the securities from the bank, it was with the intention of raiding my own office that night and leaving the sign of Four Square Jane to throw suspicion elsewhere. I came back to the office at eleven o'clock that night, but found Remington was before me. He had opened the safe with his key, and was satisfying his curiosity as to the contents of the envelopes. He threatened to expose me, for he had already discovered that the envelopes contained nothing of importance.

"I was a desperate man. I have taken a revolver with me in case I was detected, intending to end my life then and there. Remington made certain demands on me, to which I refused to agree. He rose and walked to the door, telling me he intended to call the police; it was then that I shot him."

Peter Dawes looked up from his notes.

"What about Steele's card?" he said.

Lord Claythorpe nodded.

"I had taken that with me to throw suspicion upon Steele, because I believed, and still believe, that he is associated with Four Square Jane."

"Tell me one thing," said Peter. "Do you know or suspect Four Square Jane?"

Lord Claythorpe shook his head.

"I've always suspected that she was Joyce Wilberforce herself," he said, "but I've never been able to confirm that suspicion. In the old days, when the Wilberforces were living in Manchester Square, I used to see the girl, and suspected she was carrying notes to young Steele, who had a top-floor office at the corner of Cavendish Square."

"Where were you living at the time?" asked Peter quickly.

"I had a flat in Grosvenor Square," said Lord Claythorpe.

Peter jumped up.

"Was the girl's uncle alive at this time?"

Lord Claythorpe nodded.

"He was still alive," he said.

"Where was he living?"

"In Berkeley——"

"I've got it!" said Peter excitedly. "This was when all the trouble was occurring, when you were planning to rob the girl, and using your influence against her. Don't you see? 'Four Square Jane.' She has named the four squares where the four characters in your story lived."

Lord Claythorpe frowned.

"That solution never occurred to me," he said.

He did not seem greatly interested in a matter which excited Peter Dawes to an unusual extent. He had little else to say, and when Peter Dawes left him, he lay wearily down on the plank bed.

Peter was talking for some time with the inspector in charge of the station, when the gaoler called him.

"I don't know what was the matter with that prisoner, sir," he said, "but, looking through the peephole about two minutes ago, I saw him pulling the buttons off his coat."

Peter frowned.

"You'd better change that coat of his," he said, "and place him under observation."

They all went back to the cell together. Lord Claythorpe was lying in the attitude in which Peter had left him, and they entered the cell together. Peter bent down and touched the face, then, with a cry, turned the figure over on its back.

"He's dead!" he cried.

He looked at the coat. One of the buttons had been wrenched off. Then he bent down and smelt the dead man's lips, and began a search of the floor. Presently he found what he was looking for—a section of a button. He picked it up, smelt it, and handed it to the inspector.

"So that's how he did it," he said gravely. "Claythorpe was prepared for this."

"What is it?" asked the inspector.

"The second button of his coat has evidently been made specially for him. It is a compressed tablet of cyanide of potassium, coloured to match the other buttons, and he had only to tear it off to end his life."

So passed Lord Claythorpe, a great scoundrel, leaving his title to a weakling of a son, and very few happy memories to that obscure and hysterical woman who bore his name. Peter's work was done, save for the mystery of Four Square Jane, and even that mystery was exposed. The task he had set himself now was a difficult one, and one in which he had very little heart. He obtained a fresh set of warrants, and accompanied by a small army of detectives who watched every exit, made his call at the hotel at which Steele and his wife were staying.

He went straight up to the room, and found Joyce and her husband at breakfast. They were both dressed; the fact that several trunks were packed suggested that they were contemplating an early move.

Peter closed the door behind him and came slowly to the breakfast table, and the girl greeted him with a smile.

"You're just in time for breakfast," she said. "Won't you have some coffee?"

Peter shook his head. Steele was eyeing him narrowly, and presently the young man laughed.

"Joyce," he said, "I do believe that friend Dawes has come to arrest us all."

"You might guess again, and guess wrong," said Peter, sitting himself down and leaning one elbow on the table. "Mr. Steele, the game is up. I want you!"

"And me, too?" asked the girl, raising her eyebrows.

She looked immensely pretty, he thought, and he had a sore heart for her.

"Yes, you, too, Mrs. Steele," he said quietly.

"What have I done?" she asked.

"There are several things you've done, the latest being to embrace your husband in the vestibule of the hotel when we had arrested him for being in possession of an emerald necklace, and in your emotion relieving him of the incriminating evidence."

She laughed, throwing back her head.

"It was prettily done, don't you think?" she asked.

"Very prettily," said Peter.

"Have you any other charge?"

"None, except that you are Four Square Jane," said Peter Dawes.

"So you've found that out, too, have you?" asked the girl. She raised her cup to her lips without a tremor, and her eyes were dancing with mischief.

Peter Dawes felt that had this woman been engaged on a criminal character instead of devoting her life to relieving the man who had robbed her of his easy gains, she would have lived in history as the greatest of all those perverted creatures who set the law at defiance.

Steele took a cigarette from his pocket, and offered his case to the detective.

"As you say, the jig is up," said he, "and since we desire most earnestly that there should be no unpleasant scene, and this is a more comfortable place to make a confession than a cold, cold prison cell, I will tell you that the whole scheme of Four Square Jane was mine."

"That's not true," said the girl quietly. "You mustn't take either the responsibility or the credit, dear."

Steele laughed as he held a light to the detective's cigarette.

"Anyway, I planned some of our cleverest exploits," he said, and she nodded.

"As you rightly say, Dawes, my wife is Four Square Jane. Perhaps you would like to know why she took that name?"

"I know—or, rather, I guess," said Peter. "It has to do with four squares in London."

Steele looked surprised.

"You're cleverer than I thought," he said. "But that is the truth. Joyce and I had been engaged in robbing Claythorpe for a number of years. When we got some actual, good money from him, we held tight to it. Jewels we used either to send in to the hospitals——"

"That I know, too," said Peter, and suddenly flung away his cigarette. He looked at the two suspiciously, but neither pair of eyes fell. "Now then," said Peter thickly. "Come along. I've waited too long."

He rose to his feet and staggered, then took a halting step across the room to reach the door, but Steele was behind him, and had pinioned him before he went two paces. Peter Dawes felt curiously weak and helpless. Moreover, he could not raise his voice very much above a whisper.

"That—cigarette—was—drugged," he said drowsily.

"Quite right," said Steele. "It was one of my Never Fails."

Peter's head dropped on his breast, and Steele lowered him to the ground.

The girl looked down pityingly.

"I'm awfully sorry we had to do this, dear," she said.

"It won't harm him," said Steele cheerfully. "I think we had better keep some of our sorrow for ourselves, because this hotel is certain to be surrounded. The big danger is that he's got one of his gentleman friends in the corridor outside."

He opened the door quietly and looked out. The corridor was empty. He beckoned the girl.

"Bring only the jewel-case," he said. "I have the money and the necklace in my pocket."

After closing and locking the door behind them, they passed down the corridor, not in the direction of the lift or the stairs, but towards a smaller pair of stairs, which was used as an emergency exit, in case of fire. They did not attempt to descend, but went up three flights, till they emerged on a flat roof, which commanded an excellent view of the West End of London.

Steele led the way. He had evidently reconnoitred the way, and did not once hesitate. The low roof ended abruptly in a wall on to which he climbed, assisting the girl after him. They had to cross a little neck of sloping ledge, before they came to a much more difficult foothold, a slate roof, protected only by a low parapet. They stepped gingerly along this, until they came to a skylight, which Steele lifted.

"Down you go," he said, and helped the girl to drop into the room below them.

He waited only long enough to secure the skylight, and then he followed the girl through the unfurnished room into which they had dropped, on to a landing.

In the meantime, Peter's assistant had grown nervous, and had come up to the room, and knocked. Getting no answer, he had broken in the door, to find his chief lying still conscious but helpless where he had been left. The rough-and-ready method of resuscitation to which the detective resorted, shook the drugged man from his sleep, and a doctor, hastily summoned, brought him back to normality.

He was still shaky, however, when he recounted the happenings.

"They haven't passed out of the hotel, that I'll swear," said the detective. "We're watching every entrance, including the staff entrance. How did it occur?"

Peter shook his head.

"I went like a lamb to the slaughter," he said, smiling grimly. "It was the promise of a confession, and my infernal curiosity which made me stay—to smoke a doped cigarette, too!" He thought a moment. "I don't suppose they depended entirely on the cigarette, though," he said. "And maybe it would have been a little more unpleasant for me, if I hadn't smoked."

An hour after he was well enough to conduct personally a search of the hotel premises. From cellar to roof he went, followed by two assistants, and it was not until he was actually on the roof that he discovered any clue. It was a small piece of beadwork against the wall which the girl had climbed, and which had been torn off in her exertions. They passed along the neck, and along the sloping roof till they came to the skylight, and this Peter forced.

He found, upon descending, that he was in the premises of Messrs. Backham and Boyd, ladies' outfitters. The floor below was a large sewing-room, filled with girls who were working at their machines, until the unexpected apparition of a pale and grimy man brought an end to their labours. Neither the foreman nor the forewoman had seen anybody come in, and as it was necessary to pass through the room to reach a floor lower down, this seemed to prove conclusively to Dawes that the fugitives had not made use of this method to escape.

"The only people who have been in the upstairs room," exclaimed the foreman, "are two of the warehousemen, who went up about two minutes ago, to bring down some bales."

"Two men?" said Peter quickly. "Who were they?"

But, though he pushed his inquiries to the lower and more influential regions of the shop, he could not discover the two porters. A lot of new men had been recently engaged, said the manager, and it was impossible to say who had been upstairs and who had not.

The door porter at the wholesale entrance, however, had seen the two porters come out, carrying their somewhat awkwardly-shaped bundles on their shoulders.

"Were they heavy?" asked Peter.

"Very," said the door-keeper. "They put them on a cart, and didn't come back."

Now if there was one thing more certain than another in Peter's mind, it was that Four Square Jane did not depend entirely upon the assistance she received from her husband. Peter recalled the fact that there had once been two spurious detectives who had called on Lord Claythorpe having the girl in custody. They were probably two old hands at the criminal game, enlisted by the ingenious Mr. Steele. This proved to be the case, as Peter was to find later. And either Four Square Jane or he might have planted these two men in an adjoining warehouse with the object of rendering just that kind of assistance, which, in fact, they did render.

Peter reached the streets again, baffled and angry. Then he remembered that in Lord Claythorpe's desk was a certain bond to bearer for five hundred thousand dollars. Four Square Jane would not leave England until she had secured this; and, as the thought occurred to him, he hailed a taxi, and drove at top speed to the dead man's house.

Already the news of the tragedy which had overcome the Claythorpe's household had reached the domestics: and the gloomy butler who admitted him greeted him with a scowl as though he were responsible for the death of his master.

"You can't go into the study, sir," he said, with a certain satisfaction, "it has been locked and sealed."

"By whom?" asked Peter.

"By an official of the Court, sir," said the man.

Peter went to the study door, and examined the two big red seals.

There is something about the seal of the Royal Courts of Justice which impresses even an experienced officer of the law. To break that seal without authority involves the most uncomfortable consequences, and Peter hesitated.

"Has anybody else been here?" he asked.

"Only Miss Wilberforce, sir," said the man.

"Miss Wilberforce?" almost yelled Peter. "When did she come?"

"About the same time as the officer who sealed the door," said the butler. "In fact, she was in the study when he arrived. He ordered her out pretty roughly, too, sir," said the butler with relish, as though finding in Miss Wilberforce's discomfiture some compensation for the tragedy which had overtaken his employer. "She sent me upstairs to get an umbrella she had left when she was here last, and when I came down she was gone. The officer grumbled something terribly."

Peter went to the telephone and rang up Scotland Yard, but they had heard nothing of the sealing of the house and suggested that he should seek out the Chancery officials to discover who had made the order and under what circumstances. Only those who have attempted to disturb the routine of the Court of Chancery will appreciate the unhappy hours which Peter spent that day, wandering from master to master, in a vain attempt to secure news or information.

He went back to the house at half-past four that evening, determined to brave whatever terror the Court of Chancery might impose, and again he was met by the butler on the doorstep, but this time a butler bursting with news.

"I'm very glad you've come, sir. I've got such a lot to tell you. About half-an-hour after you'd gone, sir, I heard a ripping and tearing in the study, and I went to the door and listened. I couldn't understand what was going on, so I shouted out: 'Who's there?' And who do you think replied?"

Peter's heart had sunk at the butler's words.

"I know," he said. "It was Four Square—it was Miss Joyce Wilber-force."

"So it was, sir," said the butler in surprise. "How did you know?"

"I guessed," said Peter shortly.

"It appeared she'd been locked in quite by accident by the officer of the Court," the butler went on, "and she was having a look through his lord-ship's desk to find some letters she'd left behind."

"Of course, sir, everybody knows that Lord Claythorpe's desk is one of the most wonderful in the world. It's full of secret drawers, and I remember Miss Joyce saying once that if his lordship wanted to hide anything it would take a month to find it."

Peter groaned.

"They wanted time—of course, they wanted time!"

What a fool he had been all through! There was no need for the butler to tell him the rest of the story, because he guessed it. But the man went on.

"After a bit," he said, "I heard the key turn in the lock, and out came Miss Joyce, looking as pleased as Punch. But you should have seen the state of that desk!"

"So she broke the seals, did she?" said Peter, with gentle irony.

"Oh, yes, she broke the seals, and she broke the desk, too," said the but-ler impressively. "And when she came out, she was carrying a big square sheet of paper in her hand—a printed-on paper, like a bank note, sir."

"I know," said Peter. "It was a bond."

"Ah. I think it might have been," said the butler hazily. "At any rate, that's what she had. 'Well,' she said, 'it took a lot of finding.' 'Miss,' said I, 'you oughtn't to take anything from his lordship's study until the law——' 'Blow the law,' said she. Them was her very words—blow the law, sir."

"She's blown it, all right," said Peter, and left the house. His last hope was to block all the ports, and in this way prevent their leaving the country. However, he had no great hopes of succeeding in his attempts to hold the volatile lady whose escapades had given him so many sleepless nights.

* * * *

Two months later, Peter Dawes received a letter bearing a South Amer-ican postmark. It was from Joyce Steele.

"You don't know how sorry I am that we had to give you so much trouble," it ran; "and really, the whole thing was ridiculous, because all the time I was breaking the law to secure that which was my own. It is true that I am Four Square Jane. It is equally true that I am Four Square Jane no longer, and that henceforth my life will be blameless! And really, dear Mr. Dawes, you did much better than any of the other detectives who were put on my track. I am here with my husband, and the two friends who very kindly assisted us with our many exploits are also in South America, but at a long distance from us. They are very nice people, but I am afraid they have criminal minds, and nothing appals me more than the criminal mind. No doubt there is much that has happened that has puzzled you, and made you wonder why this, or that, or the other happened. Why, for example, did I consent to go to church with that impossible person, Francis Claythorpe? Partly, dear friend, because I was already married, and it did not worry me a bit to add bigamy to my other crimes. And partly because I made ample preparations for such a contingency, and knew that marriage was impossible. I had hoped, too, that Lord Claythorpe would give me a wedding present of some value, which hope was doomed to disappointment. But I did get a lot of quite valuable presents from his many friends, and these both Jamieson and I most deeply appreciate. Jamieson was the doctor who saw me at Lewinstein's by the way. He has been my right-hand man, and my dearest confederate. Perhaps, Mr. Dawes, you will meet us again in London, when we are tired of South America. And perhaps when you meet us you will not arrest us, because you will have taken a more charitable view of our behaviour, and perhaps you will have induced those in authority to share your view. I am tremendously happy—would you be kind enough to tell my mother that? I do not think it will cheer her up, because she is not that kind.

"I first got my idea of playing Four Square Jane from hearing a servant we once employed—a Jane Briglow—discussing the heroic adventures of some fictional personage in whom she was interested. But it was a mistake to call me 'Jane.' The 'J' stands for Joyce. When you have time for a holiday, won't you come over and see us? We should love to entertain you."

There was a P.S. to the letter which brought a wry smile to the detective's face.

"P.S. Perhaps you had better bring your own cigarettes."